P R

HOLLYWOODSKI

"Screenwriters and movie buffs beware—*Hollywoodski* touches the dark nerve of desperation and surrealism behind the glitter of show business with an icicle. You have been warned."

—Patton Oswalt, author of *Silver Screen Fiend* and
Zombie Spaceship Wasteland

"*Hollywoodski* is brilliantly existential and comedic, so funny it hurts in the place where quixotic longings, bizarre encounters, impossible situations and underdogs collide. Mathews has great soul, and his writing dazzles on every page."

—Elizabeth McKenzie, author of *Dog of the North*
and *The Portable Veblen*

"*Hollywoodski* is a glorious bender of a book, a stylish and hilarious torch song for all the faded writers in this town, still ranting and dreaming long after closing time. If you love the movies so much it breaks your heart, then you will love every page of this masterpiece by the one and only Lou Mathews."

—Jim Gavin, creator of *Lodge 49* and
author of *Middle Men*

HOLLYWOODSKI

HOLLYW

Lou Mathews

DODSKI

TIGER VAN BOOKS

Tiger Van Books

An imprint of Turner Publishing Company

Nashville, Tennessee

www.turnerpublishing.com

Cover design: M. S. Corley

Book design: William Ruoto

Library of Congress Cataloging-in-Publication Data

Names: Mathews, Lou, author.

Title: Hollywoodski / by Lou Mathews.

Description: Nashville: Tiger Van Books, 2025.

Identifiers: LCCN 2024002417 (print) | LCCN 2024002418 (ebook) | ISBN 9781684429806 (paperback) | ISBN 9781684429813 (hardcover) | ISBN 9781684429820 (epub)

Subjects: LCGFT: Novels.

Classification: LCC PS3613.A8269 H65 2025 (print) | LCC PS3613.A8269 (ebook) | DDC 813/.6—dc23/eng/20240326

LC record available at https://lccn.loc.gov/2024002417

LC ebook record available at https://lccn.loc.gov/2024002418

Printed in the United States of America

1 2 3 4 5 6 7 8 9 10

"Individual Medley" and "Oscar" were published in *ZYZZYVA*. "Gower Gulch" was published in the anthology *Dust Up*. "Written Out" was published in *Six Three Whiskey*; "La Novia" was published in *New Madrid*; "Desperate Times, Desperate Crimes," "Some Animals Are More Equal Than Others," and "Tutorial" were published in the *New England Review*; and "Hollywoodski," "Not Oliver Stone," and "Persecution Street & Hazard Avenue" were published in *Black Clock*. "Quality of Life" was published in *Catamaran* and "Bat Fat" was published in *Chicago Quarterly Review*.

The writer would like to thank the National Endowment for the Arts, the California Arts Commission, and Andrew Morse and the Kirkwood Prize Foundation for their encouragement and support.

For Miguel Sandoval

Forty-year friend and my backstage pass

"Schmucks with Underwoods."

—JACK WARNER ON WRITERS

"I make private and unfunny jokes."

—NATHANAEL WEST

"I am the fire-hydrant of the underdog."
—JAIME RUBIN, DESCRIBING HIS MISADVENTURES IN THE
SCREEN-TRADE AND, LIKE ROBERT TOWNE IN *CHINATOWN*,
STEALING A LINE WITHOUT ATTRIBUTION

*"I'm a faded screenwriter. My friends say, don't you mean
a 'failed' screenwriter, and I explain, no, poets can fail.
Screenwriters can't fail, the bar is set too low. We only fade."*
—DALE DAVIS

CONTENTS

– SOME ANIMALS ARE MORE EQUAL THAN OTHERS –

(1988)

SOME ANIMALS
ARE MORE EQUAL
THAN OTHERS

(1988)

N O MAN KNOWS HIS APOTHEOSIS. CARL JUNG SAID
that. No man knows his apotheosis, but I know mine, and
I knew it at the time. That particular deal went down in the
scrubby jungle outside of Rivas. This was in Nicaragua, in 1987. I
can tell you the day and even the hour. April 22, 1:00 p.m.—the
high point of my life.

At noon that day, the producers fired Alec Litwer-Bowen as
director. Alec had recommended a two-million-dollar line of
credit, to be spent in-country, which made sense. The US embargo made the usual studio transactions impossible. When Alec
arrived in Nicaragua, he handed a million dollars over to the
Sandinista government. It would have been a bargain; government support in the form of reliable cars, trucks, gasoline, con-
struction equipment, soldiers, helicopters, boats, sailors, extras,
and rare goods like plywood and other necessities for sets would
be worth well beyond that sum. The bonding company, which
should never have known about this transaction, got squeezed
by the Reagan administration and demanded that the producers

shut down the movie or fire Alec. They fired Alec—at least that
is what we assumed. Alec had disappeared, and the studio publicists began cranking up the creative-differences-agree-to-dis-
agree machine. It was quite a concert back in LA. The rumor
machine played a bass murmur of overdoses and breakdowns
while contracts and legal piped moral turpitude. Meantime, the
studio tried to recruit an A-, B-, or even C-list director. No one
would touch it; the bad juju taint was out on this one. I was right
place, right time. I was the writer, I was second-unit assistant director, I'd made a short, I spoke Spanish. Mostly, I was there.
They handed me the swagger stick, the metaphorical pith hel-
met and megaphone. Traditionally, a transition like this would
be noted by a newly stenciled parking space and a folding chair
with my name on the back: *Dale Davis, Director.*

Three-D was the nickname I was ready to promote, but there
was no parking space because there was no road, and the chairs
were plastic. This was Nicaragua. Sid Newman, the nominal line
producer, handed me the contract, an alleged copy of which I
hadn't read the night before, and without benefit of agent or
lawyer, I signed and initialed where Sid pointed, on the back of
his administrative assistant Kevin. Kevin whirled around when
I was done and whisked away the contract, and Sid handed me a
whistle. "You should probably have a gun," Sid said, "to get the
attention of *this* cast, but short notice." Now it was on me. Alec
was gone.

. . . .

ALEC LITWER-BOWEN WAS ONE OF THE ONLY TRUE
anarchists I have ever known. Like all true anarchists, he
loved power. Directing was the perfect job for him. Directors
need the same organizational skills as generals; making a movie

on location is very much like a military campaign. Artistes and auteurs don't last long in the jungle.

We were shooting in Nicaragua because that was where Alec wanted to be at that particular moment in history, thumbing his nose at the Reagan administration and the Contra conceit.

We were there to shoot a movie, Alec's conceit, a remake of Sam Peckinpah's *Bring Me the Head of Alfredo Garcia*.

Since I revered Peckinpah almost as much as Alec did, I had no problem cobbling together a script, which we titled *Head-In-Bag*. Alec was coming off a hit, *Clash*, the story of the rise and breakup of that seminal punk band, and every young actor in the business wanted to work with him. We picked Jesse Gallo—suitably dissolute but without it starting to show on film—to play the lead part of Benny. He was as close as we could get, in his age group, to the magnificent Warren Oates, who originated the part and inhabited it still.

I was worried about Jesse. I thought he might go Brando on me when Alec was fired, but he rolled with it, which was sane. It would be his first lead in a studio picture; he enjoyed Nicaragua and the press coverage he was getting there, filming in that supposed combat zone. He also liked me. He'd come out of equity waiver theater in Chicago, a country that revered writers, and it *was* a tasty script.

Our first day, my first day as a director, was in Rivas. We were reshooting a scene from two weeks before because TACA, the airline shuttling our film to Mexico City, had lost the film. Benny, confronted by gangsters on one side and his pleading girlfriend, Elita, on the other, had climbed a Malinché tree, carrying the head of Alfredo Garcia.

Now that Alec was gone, our director of photography, D. W. "Ducky" Doyle, explained his problems with the tree. Alec had loved that tree, insisted on it. Ducky, who saw the world in frames and available light, explained the tree's problem from a cameraman's perspective. It was a problem of framing because the tree was so wide and unbalanced. The other problem was new: the tree was now in full bloom, filled with bursting orange flowers. On camera, the blooms registered like neon, and everything else in the frame, particularly the actors, looked washed out.

I made my first decision and was thrilled to hear my whim move down the chain of command.

"Lose the Malinché," Ducky called out. Geoff, the second AD, repeated the command on his bullhorn, and the Malinché was lost. We moved on to a smaller and drabber tree, one that was easier for Jesse to climb.

The new tree, a bushy Sapodilla, was in a clearing less than fifty feet from the road and presented another set of problems. The production had been shadowed by Sandinista officials. This had been helpful, mostly. We faced no landowners' complaints, no demands for compensation by the local villagers. Police officers on motorcycles preceded our buses, garbage bags of córdobas arrived when per diems had to be paid, but the longer we were in-country, the larger the Sandinista following. We were now shooting on a weekend, and the comandantes and senators and ministers had brought their wives along. They had set up a long line of plastic chairs for the most senior couples, behind the camera but in front of the crew. The junior officers and their wives, dressed for diplomatic parties—all starched creases, braid, lace, shining fabrics, piled hair, and teetery heels—stood behind them and waited for the filming to commence. I now understood how well Alec had intimidated them. This was the most intrusive they had been.

The crew waited patiently for me to do something, and I made a mistake. I should have gone myself, but I wanted to set up and look at the framing, so I sent our assistant director, Gabriel Hernandez, a respected Mexican veteran who had worked with

Peckinpah, to request that our guests move to the opposite side of the clearing, so that the crew might do their work.

I was positioning Jesse on a likely branch, pointing out the foliage that should be trimmed, when the shouting began. I couldn't imagine Gabriel being rude, but he may have been matter-of-fact. A comandante was being restrained; there was much head-tossing and fluttering hands amongst the wives. Several ministers were yelling at Gabriel and pointing fingers in his face. I had not seen a single Nicaraguan point with a finger the whole time I'd been there. They'd point with pursed lips, they'd point with their noses, but finger-pointing was unforgivably rude.

I rushed over with Ducky and tried to make sense of it. What the comandante was continuing to scream was that no Mexican was going to tell him where to stand in his own country, as Los Chingados had been trying to do for years. Maricón Mexicanos were also mentioned, and Chilangos.

"It's that kick-down thing," Ducky said. The Nicaraguan perception was that Mexicans respected Cubans a bit and Costa Ricans somewhat. Everyone else in Central America, particularly Nicaraguans, were considered kickable. "We need to apologize," Ducky said. "Don't make them move. We'll move the camera and shoot from the other side."

I apologized for the misunderstanding and breach of manners. Gabriel was hustled away, water and snacks were brought, and things settled down.

We set up on the other side, the crew hustling so that we wouldn't lose the light, and nailed it in two takes. Each time I called "Cut," the Sandinistas applauded. We packed up and got the hell out, heading for the coast.

We moved, cast and crew, to San Juan del Sur, a disheveled beach town with unspoiled beaches to the south, where we would film scenes of Benny washing ashore with the head of Alfredo Garcia.

The Sandinista brass, military and civilian, moved with us. They liked moviemaking, and they enjoyed the long pauses between actions, when they had time to talk to unoccupied actors. The actors were charming and interested. The law, established by Alec, was maintained: Anyone with a uniform or an aide was treated like a producer. Since it was no longer the weekend, they were unaccompanied by their wives, and the drinking started earlier.

All of the Sandinista cohort, the stuntmen, and most of the crew stayed at the air-conditioned government hotel on the hill above the town, the Barlovento. Most of the cast followed me to the Estrella, a reeling two-story wood and tin-roofed hotel across from the beach. Tennessee Williams would have loved the joint. It was not so much painted as smeared with a copper-based green primer that the owners loved because the paint job had lasted now for two rainy seasons. The owners, Roberto and Alma Huesca, had inflated their rates for the movie-company visit to thirty thousand córdobas, a little less than three dollars a night. Men slept six to a room on the second floor. The women were lodged downstairs in a chain-linked, chain-locked purdah enclosure. For Roberto and Alma, it was a matter of Catholic propriety and insurance. The wardrobe mistress, Colleen Regan, inspected the fence and the locks and announced that she felt "Extremely valued. It's the first time any of you ponces have shown us the respect we deserve. We deserve to be locked up; we *should* be locked up. We are sexy and dangerous and need to be caged. Just please do not tell me that I cannot drink or smoke in my cage the way that any proper English budgie is allowed."

That first night, we all went up to the Barlovento for dinner and festivities. The usual poker game had commenced with foot-high stacks of córdobas in front of each player. Two grips, Ducky Doyle, two extras, and Jesse. They were letting Jesse win, as I had instructed and offered to pay for. I wanted him to be in a good mood for the important shot in the morning. Jesse was nodding and beaming, two toppling stacks of bills in front of him. Candles and kerosene lanterns gave a romantic cast to the scene, but it wasn't by choice. The entire hotel was lit by candles and lanterns. The power had cut off a little after seven. An announcement was made that this was the result of yet another attack by the Contras on power lines. Some of the newly arrived were thrilled. The locals, used to their power company's on-demand maintenance, were not. The hotel's backup generator wouldn't start. Two Sandinista colonels supervised the attempt. A half hour into the procedure, they'd taken over from the very nervous maintenance crew. One had poured 151-proof rum down the throat of the carburetor while the other pulled the starter rope. The resulting backfire set the machine ablaze and all watched, exultant, as it burned, helped by thrown copitas of rum, whenever the fire died down.

The ice crisis started around midnight. Most of us were drinking beers by that time, which had stayed reasonably luke-cold in the quiescent refrigerators, but the two colonels who had set the generator on fire had commandeered the bar's blenders, which they hooked up, with adapters, to car batteries. They were blending and sending pitchers of sweetened rum and fruit drinks to the women of the cast and crew. The drinks were standard—piña coladas, banana, mango, papaya, and guanabana daiquiris—but they were delivered by hand, by the bowing colonels, with titles: *Daiquiri Mi Amor, Piña besos, Mango-a-go-go!*

By midnight, the bar was out of ice. The colonels had the hotel manager awakened, and the reserves of ice, which had been banked around the fish, shrimp, and shellfish in the big freezer to keep them fresh through the power outage, were confiscated. Most of the actresses left after the second or third batch of slightly shrimpy piña coladas, but the sturdier girls of design, hair, makeup, and wardrobe remained, and by one even the confiscated ice was gone.

The colonels demanded more ice. The hotel manager had wisely driven himself and his family down the hill. One of the colonels remembered the full and operative refrigerator freezer, with the generator that never failed, nearby at a confiscated Somocista mansion, the love nest of the reviled Anastasio Somoza, not more than twenty kilometers away. They demanded transport. Instantly!

The hotel staff and even the junior officers had scattered by now, even the drunkest having sensed the tidally swelling danger. There was no question of the colonels driving themselves. They were triumphantly drunk, and their car batteries had been killed by blenders.

Only Solano remained, loyal Solano. Solano was one of the first taxi drivers the production company had hired. He was assigned to the production designer, Horacio O'Reilly. Horacio, UCLA-trained but Peruvian-born, understood what it meant to be a patrón, and the first thing he asked Solano was what would he like from the United States. Solano asked for a typewriter. He wanted to be a writer. George Orwell, Lorca, and Ruben Dario were his heroes. Horacio provided both an electric Smith-Corona and a manual Olivetti for the power outages. Typewriters delivered, Solano awaited Horacio's whim, night and day, until the end of days, to the gates of hell.

Solano, small, meek, dressed in his all-purpose white-and-silver-striped track suit, was napping on a sofa next to the dining room when the senior colonel, Onofre Buendia, came roaring in. "My driver is gone!" the colonel shouted. "I need another driver to get me ice. You!" He pointed to Solano, who sat up from the sofa like a mole trapped in the sun. His small fists scrubbed his eyes.

A kind of dialogue followed. Solano asked if Don Horacio had ordered this. The colonel insisted on ice. Solano agreed, nodding, of course, "As long as Don Horacio gives me permission."

"We are leaving," the colonel shouted. "Fuck that Mexican, Horacio."

"Of course," Solano said, nodding, almost bowing. "As long as Don Horacio says so." The colonel nudged his pistol against Solano's ear.

I had been sleeping in a booth in the dining room and awakened to the shout of, "Ice. You!"

By the time I tottered forward, Solano was on his knees, the colonel was cocking his .45, the blunt, square barrel against Solano's forehead, and I did what I thought needed to be done.

"Solano!" I barked. The colonel wheeled on me, the .45 very much alive in his hand. "Solano," I said. "Go and get the car."

The colonel looked at me, squinting and sideways. "I am the director," I said.

He straightened. "I know who you are. That is not important." But it was. The gun had left Solano's forehead.

"Go and get the colonel's car," I told Solano.

The colonel gave me a wobbly smile, and his arm dropped. He sat down in one of the springy leather booths and spread like spilled pudding, as though he had just lost many bones. "These people," he said.

"Let me take care of this," I said.

I followed Solano out to the parking area, to his tattered Datsun, and we fled.

We hid the car under a canvas, in a boat shed near the beach, and, with special dispensation, we ourselves hid in the depths of the women's padlocked lower confine of the Estrella. There, surrounded by fragrant, drunken, lightly snoring women on the cots above us, terrified as we were, Solano and I went to sleep. Solano made only one comment, when it seemed we had escaped. "It is as they say." He held up the book he kept in the glove box to read while he waited, George Orwell's *Granja de Animales*. "Some animals are more equal than others."

At dawn, Monday, the Sandinista brass were gone, and so were our superiors from the studio and the line producers. The company assembled, and we went to shoot the scenes that turned out to be our last.

A week before, in the still waters of Lake Managua, Alec Litwer-Bowen had shot his last scene. Benny, whirling the bag containing the head of Alfredo Garcia like a blackjack, had knocked out his guard and jumped from the deck of the gangster's yacht into the Pacific Ocean.

A week later, in the ruffled surf of the actual Pacific Ocean, on a wild beach where driftwood etched through a fog, we completed the action. We shot nine takes of Benny rolling ashore with the head of Alfredo Garcia. Gorgeous stuff. We spent the rest of the day in the jungle on a series of chase shots and gunfire through the trees.

The newly cut road back to San Juan was so rough that most of the cast, who had suffered the drive out, elected to walk the three kilometers back to San Juan along the beach. By the time we got back, at sundown, they'd pulled the plug on the picture.

Sid Newman delegated, which didn't surprise me. Not Sid, but his administrative assistant Kevin, met us at the Estrella. He had elaborately organized transport schedules, per diems, plane tickets, waivers, and checks; the checks were handed over once the waivers were signed.

Kevin was a regular little company asshole for a while. He wouldn't talk to me. Said I was a special case and was to sit tight until tomorrow, when Sid would arrive and inform me of my status. As director of a defunct movie. I didn't need Sid to tell me that.

Kevin finally got shifted when he was persuading Tyrell "Crack Back" Tyler to sign his waiver. Crack Back, before he'd started acting, had been a twelve-year outside linebacker for the Bears, and Kevin was Chicago born and bred. He worshipped the man.

While Crack Back was signing and initialing where Kevin pointed, Kevin chattered on about what a huge Bears fan he was, and what a Crack Back fan he had been as a kid.

Crack Back signed the last page, guaranteeing that he would not sue any of the twelve named producers, the studio, or the US government, or ever talk about the alleged movie, and looked hard at Kevin. "You from Chicago?" Crack Back stood up.

"Totally," Kevin said.

"Then why the fuck," Crack Back wondered aloud, "are you siding with the enemy? We had a good movie to make here. Been a change in persona for me." Crack Back was cast as a hit man, with gay overtones, the Gig Young part in the original. Kevin wilted. He covered his head and started to rock and sway.

Crack Back headed for the shuttle back to Managua. The shuttle driver held open the door. "¡Vamanos!" Crack Back said. That surprised me. The man had lived eight weeks in Nicaragua and learned only one Spanish phrase, "Como se llama, Mama?"

Kevin was stricken. Once he'd collected his last set of signatures and locked them in the hotel safe at the Barlovento, he fell apart. After his fourth Nica Libré, he told me what he knew.

The Reaganistas had sources *very* high up in the Sandinista government. They knew about Alec's contribution to the local economy before the studio did. The squeeze had started from on high and down low.

A number of tax audits were initiated; some studio tax credits that had gone unquestioned in previous years got questioned. One French director and one English actress, who were scheduled to film the studio's "quality" picture for the year, were denied visas. Those were some of the sticks.

Then the carrots were dangled. Whatever losses the studio might incur for shutting down *Head-In-Bag*—and they would be small, since it was a negative pickup deal—would be more than offset by the lack of scrutiny on a studio merger that had major antitrust implications.

It seemed like shooting a flea with an elephant gun to me, but things had heated up on the Honduran border. A CIA pilot had been captured with a load of Contra arms when his plane crashed in Nicaragua, and then a nice California kid, Benjamin Linder, had been killed by the Contras in the small northern village where he taught kids to ride a unicycle and introductory clown and mime. Also, the reporters who had followed us during the shoot were presenting a picture of Nicaragua that was not as threatening as the Reaganista version. They wanted us gone and the memory of us fading. It wouldn't be hard.

"I'm really sorry," Kevin said. "I know it would have been a good movie. I can't believe Crack Back Tyler hates me."

I nodded. "Maybe I can help there. I'll tell him it wasn't your fault. One thing he'd like to know, and so would I, is do you know what happened to the footage we've already shot?"

"Oh, man," Kevin said. "Oh, man. That was fucked up. They refused to pay for processing." All of our footage had gone to Mexico City to be developed and processed. When the studio refused to pay for processing, Ciné Allianza had exposed and tossed the film. None of us would even have a frame to add to our reels. Nothing we had filmed would exist beyond memory. We'd done theatre.

It was a Friday. The seventh of May. Most of the crew, stunts, and production took the first shuttles to Managua. About half the cast and a quarter of the crew stayed on for one last night together in San Juan del Sur. We were banned from the Barlovento. The producers refused to pay the suddenly inflated governmental rates, and the Sandinistas weren't happy with us on a personal and political level. We all shifted to the Estrella, which was exactly the right place to be at that particular time. We parked our bags and walked across the street to the beach.

Nobody slept much. Beach naps between swims. Dinner arrived, serially, from the palapa restaurants on the beach. As fish were unloaded from the boats, they were gutted, scaled, grilled over a wood fire, doused in the surf, grilled on the other side, doused again, and delivered, with black beans, fried plantains, and lime and mango salsa. The fish was charred, flaky, and delicious, seasoned only with the ocean. Saffron rice and skewers of shrimp came next, along with the sympathetic staff of the Barlovento who still liked us. Someone at a farm well away from town had been informed that Los Yanquis had lost their jobs—which was true—assumed we were hungry, roasted a pig, and carried it to town on a heroic litter, with roasted corn and small, uncharacteristic tamales filled with raisins and citron. The Barlovento staff brought us beer in washtubs filled with ice, bottles of Flor de Caña were passed, and the feast was laid out on a thatched tablecloth of banana leaves on the sand. The blenders in the palapa restaurants whirled continually, and pitchers of mango, papaya, pineapple, banana, guava, guanabana, and lime juice arrived. There was no ice, aside from the washtubs, and no one cared.

We moved to the Estrella around two. It was pleasant on the beach, but the wind carried the music away, and we craved closeness on our last night, and intensity. Nearly thirty people squeezed into a room for six, the largest upstairs dormer room, singing, stomping out the beat on the floor. There was some real talent in that room: three guitars, a mandolin, a saxophone, tambourines, maracas, and bongos.

We went through our Motown phase, Chicago Blues phase, Bo Diddley, Otis Redding, then all twenty-six verses of Marty Robbins's "El Paso." That took us almost two hours to complete, because every time we blew a verse, Ducky Doyle, our formerly gentle director of photography, made us drink a shot and start over. He became a martinet, dictating beats and pauses with a rolled-up *Barricada* newspaper. If you jumped a verse, he whacked you back into time.

Outside on the street, the locals who couldn't crowd into the room with us clapped and sang along. Around three, while we were singing "Peggy Sue," everyone started stomping so hard, in unison, that the flaking paint jumped off the walls; you could feel the joists and the walls and the floors below us bouncing and shaking.

Kevin, of all people, finally got us to sing his favorite, Bo Diddley's "Who Do You Love?" In his high, reedy, but true tenor, Kevin sang, "Tombstone hand and a graveyard mind. Just twenty-two and I don't mind dying." And when we all had swung into the chorus, "Who do you love? Who do you love?" Kevin started to cry. I hoped the moment would stay with him, but I didn't think it would, and another side of me knew he would get over it fast. He had a future in the business.

At the survivor's breakfast on the beach—fruit, leftover tamales, and, miraculously, coffee—one of the extras, a Bakersfield kid named Sacha Howells, who had been a Quaker volunteer in the north, came up to me, grinning. "You guys should go into the exterminating business."

He'd been staying at a hostel up the street, and we'd made so much noise he couldn't sleep. He came down to stand in the street with the rest of the crowd.

"Around three," Sacha said, "when you really got going, that whole building started to sway. It was bouncing before, but then it started to sway. When it started moving side to side, the cucarachas and geckos and snakes started crawling out of the eaves and dropping into the street. When you started on 'Who Do You Love?' the rats started running out the front door and diving out the windows. Look, take a look there." He pointed to a concrete pipe across the street, beside the Estrella. There were a lot of small furry bodies in the shadows. "If the place don't fall down today," Sacha said, "they can sell it as the only bug-free, rat-free hotel in San Juan del Sur."

Sid Newman arrived that morning, ready for the day in a way we survivors never could be. He got nearly everyone else onto the Last FREE Shuttle to Managua—and that was the way he described it—by four in the afternoon. After that, it was understood, the Decliners—the term he used—were on their own.

Sid had waivers for me to sign, and when I wouldn't, he sat and tried to reason. "Look," Sid said, "the studio won't hold any of this against you. It wasn't your fuckup. They just need to know you won't be part of whatever trouble Alec tries to stir up stateside. I can't promise anything, but I think they may have something in mind for you when you get back. And I'll tell you, Alec doesn't have anything good to say about you."

I knew all that was probably true, except the part about the studio having something in mind for me. Alec probably was poor-mouthing me, but I still cared about the movie we didn't get to make, and if I got the chance to tell my side of it, I would. I have been accused, in the past, of having an exaggerated sense of justice and fair play. Which meant that I still believed in the concept.

I declined, and Sid invoked the magic phrase again. "On your own," Sid said. He handed me my plane tickets, which were for a TACA flight, leaving in a week.

"Can I get an earlier flight?"

Sid smiled. "You can try. If you got cash. You can't turn these in."

I got the gist. They wanted me in-country, until there wouldn't be any press reception awaiting my arrival. A week would be enough.

Kevin minded me for two days and then handed me off to a low-level Sandinista press officer, a would-be poet named Dionisio. Kevin had been the stable goat; once I was considered secure,

Dionisio was good enough. Neither Sid nor Kevin, nor any of the Sandinista hierarchy, informed Dionisio as to what I had been doing in-country. He only knew that I was a writer and handled me as a journalista. Dionisio seemed to have the impression that I had just arrived and gave me the tour. I didn't have the heart to disabuse him. I was pretty numb by then and along for the ride.

Dionisio showed me the famous volcanoes. We had a voyage on Lake Managua, and he expressed an interest in the freshwater sharks that we didn't see. He was baffled by his superiors' lack of interest in his poetry. On my last day in Nicaragua, we visited Maria Soledad, the novia de Augusto Sandino, which affected Dionisio so strongly that he had to abandon me at a restaurant, *El Volcan*, outside Managua. I took two taxis to the airport, the second after the first dropped a driveshaft near the memorial to the Heroes of the Revolución.

I sat in the shadowed recesses of the airport, on a backless bench in a corrugated iron building that had been built and re-built on the architectural principle of lean-to sheds, and waited for my flight to Mexico City, which was now delayed four hours incoming from Mexico City.

The afternoon rains had commenced, drumming like cavalry on the metal roof. The wet season began in late April, and the rain came down on schedule—two to five, every afternoon. It was startling, the first time. The taxi I was in had rusted-out floors, and when we hydroplaned into a dip and stalled, the water crept up beyond the floors and we had to crouch on the seat until the rain stopped. It was monumental, pounding rain, drops the size of tennis balls with a noise and fury that made you believe in an Old Testament God.

We had arrived in April, to shoot in the dry season. The first day, when we left Managua, the poverty of the place hit us like a fist. In our half-full chartered bus on the road to Granada we passed hundreds of hitchhikers—soldiers, small children, schoolgirls in uniform, women on their way to market with baskets and bundles, well-dressed men and women, some carrying briefcases. The traffic slowed to a crawl as cars stacked up behind overloaded buses and open trucks, smoking and laboring on the slightest grade. Passengers clung to the sides and roofs, bumpers, and side mirrors and hung out the open windows and doors, anyplace they could get a handhold.

It was the dry season and the burning season. Sugar cane, Nicaragua's main crop, was slash-and-burn farming. Everywhere there were fires: fires in the fields, cooking fires inside dark houses, brush fires in gullies, inexplicable fires in ditches along the road and spilling from the shoulder to the roadway.

I thought the rainy season would somehow cleanse all that, but it didn't. The sun was always behind those clouds and once the rain had stopped, the scent of poverty—woodsmoke, shit, and the dead fish of dead Lake Managua—would return. A fetid atmosphere took the place of the sharp smells of the dry season. The rain was rolling now, marching over the roof in cadence. At the airport bar, the only patrons, three soldiers with AK-47s propped against the bar, looked up as it reached its crescendo, and then they returned to their beers. It was a true Nicaraguan tableau. The three soldiers, boys really, maybe sixteen, sipped their beers through straws punched into plastic bags. It startled me, the first time I saw this in the market at Masaya. I thought I was seeing boys carrying urine samples, until I saw them drink. After the revolution, the bottling plants shut down while the owners moved to Miami to nurture their portfolios until a sensible government returned. Beer was cheap, bottles were precious, and bartenders automatically poured your purchase into a bag unless you wanted to pay a premium—three times the price of the beer. They were genuinely nice people, Nicaraguans. I hated that we had held out some hope to them.

I sat there, in that airport in Managua, surrounded by the

odors of rotting fruit and the fungicides they sprayed on incoming passengers, knowing that I was as far away and as exotic as I would ever be. I dreaded boarding the plane because once I did, I would no longer be in-country. I would no longer be even a fired director.

The three boy soldiers had finished their beers and come out into the courtyard behind the terminal. They leaned their AK-47s against the wall and went to the edge of the courtyard to piss on the trunk of a Malinché tree, dropping its orange blossoms on the cobbles. Boys need a target.

The whole time I was in Nicaragua, I tried to get someone to explain to me why this particular tree was called a Malinché. In Florida, in Cuba, in Puerto Rico, in the tropical regions of Mexico, the tree is called a Flamboyan. Only in Nicaragua is it called a Malinché, and no one could explain why. In Mexico, Malinché is a cursed word, the name of the woman who accompanied Hernán Cortés in his conquests.

It would be six more hours before the plane that would take me to Mexico City would arrive, refuel, and turn around. In two more hours, I could enjoy the leatherette seats of the Mexico City airport and one-dollar bottles of Bohemia with a glass, and then there would be a four-and-a-half-hour flight on Aeromexico to Los Angeles, all the time knowing that when I touched down, I would be just another writer in turn-around.

- GOWER GULCH -

(2004)

GOWER GULCH

(2004)

———————

I LIKE THE POWER BREAKFAST AT DENNY'S. ABOUT two in the afternoon when the heavy hitters are gone and it's just me and the philosophers. This is a famous Denny's, corner of Sunset and Gower, the first 24-hr Denny's. Jim Morrison used to pass out here. Andy Kaufman used to bus tables here.

It's across from what used to be Columbia Pictures, now Sunset-Gower Studios, and that lends a certain wistfulness to the whole scene. You have a whole lot of people who shouldn't have any hope at all who got some once making big money at the studio. They're not over it yet. One of the things that worries me in this modern age is that a lot of people survive who shouldn't. They all come to Denny's. They should've been left out on a rock like the Aztecs did. Instead, they're ordering skillet breakfasts and taking up space.

There are two guys at the booth behind me who should have been chained to those rocks long ago. One of them is eating a skillet breakfast, which is a sure sign of stupidity because those are not cooked to order; the other, Al, isn't eating. He's worried about his stomach. He's got ice water into which he's poured half-and-half. I watch him stir it in the mirrored sidewall segmented by appliqué Oscar statues to remind us where we reside.

The one working on the farmer skillet pretty good is Petey Powell, who was a bad child actor thirty years ago. He's not even in reruns now, but he has cards that have his sixteen-year-old visage, and he likes to pass them out in lieu of tips. Petey, in his wisdom, says to Al, "Maybe you should have some coffee. You want some coffee?"

Al says, "Naw, naw. No more coffee. I'm too tense, you know."

Al hasn't had anything to make him tense since he got disability, twelve years ago, but Petey takes him seriously, which tells you a lot about Petey. "That's LA," he says, "That's the pressure."

Al stirs up his milky ice water. "I'm just sort of jangled."

"Yeah?" Petey says. "Maybe you should learn to meditate. You want me to teach you how to meditate?"

Al does a double take so hard his chins quiver. "You? Teach me? Are you kidding? I've been meditating since I was eight."

"You don't need no help? You know already."

"You don't know about me? I'm famous for that." Al pauses in a way that lets you know that he's said this a lot. "As a meditator, I'm a mother fucker."

Petey picks up his skillet to scrape the last of the potatoes. Al finally sees me watching. "Shut up, Davis," he tells me. "I know what you're thinking."

Petey says, "Whut?" and Al says, "Just ignore him," which Petey successfully does and always will because he's got that actor thing going.

Al smooths his palm over his heartburn and then pats himself. "Meditator? I'm a regular Buddha."

"You look like him," Petey says. Every once in a while, Petey can surprise you. Al has a superb beer belly.

"You probably don't know this," Al says. "I was born on Buddha's birthday. May second. That's a true fact."

Petey thinks about this—either that or he's out of potatoes, because he's paused.

"Know who else was born on May second?" Al says.

"May second," Petey says carefully.

"So was Harry Truman. May second. Figure that one out. The guy who dropped the atomic bomb."

Petey thinks this over for a while, and you can tell he's really concentrating this time because he's scratching his sideburn with his fork. "That makes sense to me," Petey says. "I mean, when you think about it, they both wanted peace."

I'm pretty quiet about it, but a small snort escapes and the coffee is coming out my nose.

Not looking at me, looking up at the ceiling, Al says, "Shut up, Davis. If you knew what you were doing, you wouldn't be here."

- HOLLYWOODSKI -

(2008)

HOLLYWOODSKI

(2008)

COULD BE THE OLYMPICS. JAIME RUBIN LIFTS HIS empty glass to torch-height, hoists what he thinks are his famously emphatic eyebrows, and bawls toward Kenny the Bartender, "Yo, Kelsoe! A round for the house! Davis is buying!"

There are at least three things wrong with that declaration. Kenny the Bartender's last name is Ishikawa, which does not accord with Jaime's theory that all bartenders should be named *Kelsoe*, just as all dogs should be named *Spot*, all cats should be named *Puff*, and all fuckups, male or female, should be named *Ace*, as in, "Way to go, *Ace*!," which is the slogan Jaime likes to recite when fuckups occur. Jaime, which he pronounces "Hymie," has a lot of theories. He has developed them over the years, entertaining himself and, he insists, casts and crews, on many, many sets. He now believes that when he is hired, so rarely, it is mainly because of the memories of his eccentric character and those theories. I don't argue with that. What I say to Jaime is, "Eccentricity. Theories. That makes actual sense. You're right. No one is going to hire you for your writing skills." To which Jaime will always reply, "Fuck you, Union Steward. At least I knew when to quit." Which shuts me up. I still can't talk about that. I will instead talk about the honey-colored light that filters into Bowdler's in the forenoon. The whole back bar has a glow to it, and the liqueurs on the top shelf look like the fake but well-lit jewels in *King Solomon's Mines*, although Oscar says the reference should be *The Man Who Would Be King*—faker jewels but better movie. Jaime always votes for *20,000 Leagues Under the Sea*, which is about the same level movie as *King Sol* but with vaults of jewels aboard the Nautilus; what kicks it for Jaime is that the jewels are used as ballast.

The second thing is not actually wrong, it's more of an exaggeration. "A round for the house!" should be a ringing declaration. That declaration should register and impress. And it would, except that the house, as currently configured, is me—that's Dale Davis—Jaime Rubin, and another faded writer, Oscar Grunfeld. "Faded" is my choice, and Oscar, as always, objects. I explain that we don't have "failed" writers in television—that's reserved for poets who fail honorably. Oscar brings up his chapbook and major screen credit for the noir classic *Forty-Two Pickup*. I remind him of *My Mother the Car*, a one-season show that Oscar worked on. Movie and television writers don't fail—it is impossible to fail; the bar is set too low. We fade.

It is now nearly one o'clock on the day shift here at Bowdler's, a direct reversal from one o'clock on the night shift, when there are women and fruit drinks, designer vodkas, triple-distilled vodkas, French vodkas, laughter, noise, attractive women, and dim lighting, which makes the *Signature Showcase (t.m.) Bowdler's Bartender Move* even more impressive. A ten-yard ribbon of lighter fluid around three corners of the bar. *Flick!* The blue streak, shock and awe. Invented at Bowdler's. There are bartenders at The Powerhouse, Barney's Beanery and both Frolic Rooms who also claim the invention, but they can't document, and Bowdler's can. April 7, 1938, the *Hollywood Herald*: "Bartender Adolph Kelsoe lit up the room last night at Bowdler's..." Jaime carries a laminated copy of the clipping.

The daytime is different. The back bar does glow, and the liqueurs on the top shelf do look like jewels, but when the back door is opened, the shocking white light blasts in on the shrinking mole people, the dust motes hang in that white light, and you see once again the grubby astroturf and molded white plastic chairs of what Bowdler's insists is a *patio*. There is a dead ficus tree in a clay pot there. Some broken Mission-style roof tiles. That doesn't make it a patio. No Spanish colonial emphasis will make it so. Bad set design. In the Guatemalan jungle, which I once visited for the filming of *Carnosaur*, the ficus trees reached eighty feet and were known as the *palo de mata*. The tree of death, or strangler fig. Twining parasites, they enwrap and consume their host, much like producers and directors and actors as they absorb and digest an original story and make it their own. Not that we are bitter. *Palo de mata*, that was south of Tikal, the one Maya site that everyone knows, the Rebel Base in *Star Wars*, and don't ask me which one in the sequence. Let's just say the only good one, the first one, the Rebel Base, two pyramids popping out of the jungle. Guys in segmented plastic armor, on top of the pyramids, with spears? What's that about?

The third thing that is wrong with Jaime Rubin's attempt to order another round is that Davis is supposed to be buying. But Davis is not buying because Davis is not working. And Jaime knows that, and knows, for God's sake, that I am the one who started that tradition. It was after a lunch with actors at the Beachwood Cafe. My first week on staff at Paramount and five of us around the table, me and four actors. The check came and Bill Hootkins—bless his large heart, dead now—grabbed it and went around the table, pointing: "You workin'? You workin'? You workin'?" Those who were working, me and Luis Contreras, also now dead and bless his heart, paid the check, but what I loved in the moment was that there was no stigma to *not working*, and implicit was the understanding that next week when we met again for lunch, two or three entirely different people might pay the check. We never actually did meet again for lunch, or at least I was not invited, but I loved that sentiment. Actors, greatest people in the world—as long as they're working. You don't want to be around them when they're not working. They brood on the injustices of the world. Most of these injustices involve the abuse of worthy, deserving, naive, principled, and idealistic actors. A lot of the damage done in this world is done by thwarted artists. Hitler, bad watercolorist; Goering, would-be composer; and Goebbels, bad novelist and playwright, come to mind.

Kenny the Bartender licks a finger and turns the page on the paperback he is reading beneath the cash register light. Something by Philip K. Dick. Kenny has taste. Bless his heart, he keeps a small shelf of books next to the register, written by Bowdler's patrons, alive and dead. Jim Thompson, Nathanael West, F. Scott, Budd Schulberg. He also has a number of writers you've never heard of, the ones he describes as underappreciated. I am on that list. Kenny keeps a copy of my lone hardback novel, *Treading Water*, on the shelf.

"Kelsoe, my good man!" Jaime brays, an aggrieved and plaintive note. Kenny doesn't look up, emphatically. There is no waitress during the day, which means that Jaime is stuck. At night, our usual waitress, a lifer named Sherry, will answer to Gloria—which is Jaime's designated name for all cocktail waitresses—and take Jaime's order. Kenny will *sometimes* answer to Kelsoe but mainly not, and never when he is reading literary fiction.

I stopped doing the night shift at Bowdler's a while back. It's bad enough to be invisible when looking for work; I hate being invisible for recreational purposes. What I say is, I prefer days, with no waitress, because at least then I get some exercise. This is one of those times.

Jaime holds a hand up to his cheek, as though he's just been slapped, stung and shocked by Kenny's impertinent behavior. "You saw it, Gillespie," he says to Oscar.

"I saw it," Oscar says. Jaime stares, eyes bugged.

"What are you going to do?"

Oscar tosses back the last of his crème de menthe and says, "I don't know."

Jaime puts a tremble in his voice. "There was a time," he says, pointing to Kenny, "when I could have had you shot!"

"*In the Heat of the Night*," Oscar says. "Nineteen sixty-seven. Stirling Silliphant. John Ball novel. A good one, but what Endicott *actually* says is, 'I'll remember that.' He says that to Sheriff Gillespie, and *then* he turns to Virgil Tibbs and says, 'There was a time...'"

I stand up and get my exercise, walking the long way around to the bar. "Kenny," I say. "May we have the usual, please."

Kenny puts down his book and pours, brandy and soda in a tall glass for me, crème de cacao for Oscar. He has a progression, Oscar: Cointreau, then Grand Marnier, crème de menthe, crème de cacao. If he lasts till evening, then Green Chartreuse, Yellow Chartreuse, then Kahlua. Oscar is a stately Seven-level Pousse Café when he lasts, befitting the only rich man among us, the only one who owns real estate. Jaime gets a house vodka martini, two olives and an onion and fresh ground pepper. Kenny actually keeps a pepper grinder behind the bar and turns it for Jaime. Jaime refuses to buy into Name vodka because he once researched—not wrote, researched—a Russian war epic and dealt with revolutionary-era generals who doused their vodka with pepper. When he asked, why the pepper, the Soviet generals said, to draw off the fusel oils. *All vodka is shit, distilled from poisons. Desperate times, 1916, we was draining alcohol from torpedoes and lanterns, the pepper draw off the poisons.*

Maybe the vodka got better, but by then they liked the taste of pepper, so they kept drinking that way. So did Jaime. Another determined eccentricity. He's glad to explain it to you.

I bring Oscar his crème de cacao and set my brandy and soda down, go back for Jaime's overloaded martini into which Kenny is ceremoniously grinding pepper. "This one is on Jaime's tab," I tell Kenny, though I really don't have to. First round is mine, Jaime gets the second, Oscar as the rich man buys the third and fourth. This was ordained long ago. Today, however, because Jaime is fucking with us and the world, he has to stand up, waggling a hand. "Di' he jus' say to poot it own my tab?" I am pretty sure Jaime is trying to channel Al Pacino in *Scarface*, doing the worst Cuban/Puerto Rican accent in the history of the world. Kenny doesn't care. He writes the numbers in Jaime's tab and goes back to his book. Jaime absorbs this and changes gears. He wanders in the darkness away from the table, gathering himself, and comes back, coiled. He sits in his chair, for an instant, and then explodes out of it, sideways, with his left hand on his hip, his right hand pointing. "Kenny!" Jaime shouts. "I owe you money!"

It's a variant, a good one, and Oscar recognizes it immediately.

"George C. Scott," Oscar says, "*The Hustler.* Nineteen sixty-one. Robert Rossen. Great movie, great adaptation, and sad proof that a complete son-of-a-bitch can write a great script." Oscar goes back to the blacklist days, and there are certain things we can't argue with him. "Bingo!" Jaime says and lifts his martini.

To understand Jaime, you have to understand where he's coming from, which is about 1975. His hero was Lorenzo Semple Jr. Jaime was at the Squaw Valley Writers Conference in 1975, a scholarship student in poetry, and vulnerable. Lorenzo had a huge impact on Jaime. Not always favorable.

I have to back up here. I was at that same conference; that's where Jaime and I met. I was on my way to UC Irvine in fiction, Jaime in poetry, before he was derailed by Lorenzo Semple Jr. We shared a cabin. Jaime had to take the top bunk and bring in the firewood because this was my second time at Squaw Valley and his first.

Lorenzo Semple Jr. was an impressive man. He is probably still alive; he had that radioactive capability, like Keith Richards, capable of outliving and suing us all. He was a major, *major* cult screenwriter. *Pretty Poison* you know. *Parallax View* would make him famous at film schools; the screening test for sociopaths, that alone would have kept him famous among screenwriters for a hundred years. We all passed. He was on his way to *Papillon* and *King Kong*—he thrilled us with Dino De Laurentis's explanation for the twenty-million-dollar financing for *King Kong*, "Evereabody likea da Big Monkey."

At that exact moment he was coming off an uncredited, but he suggested, obscenely well-paid, contribution to the script of *White Dawn*. Phil Kaufman movie, a good one, difficult and underrated director. You may have noticed that we don't talk much about *auteurs* here. For a reason. We talk about *primary artists* here at Bowdler's. Fastest way to end a Hollywood party is to ask the guests whether they know the definition of a *primary artist*.

Once you explain that the term only refers to those with original ideas—novelists, short story writers, poets, playwrights, painters, sculptors—there is a puzzled silence. When you go on to explain that *secondary artists* are people like actors, directors, costume designers, focus pullers, grips, agents, and honey-bucket drivers—those who mouth the words of *primary artists*, the rush for the door begins. I lost my fourth wife, Aimee I think, in that rush; she left with a grip on a grip. Steady work.

If you look at the credits for *White Dawn*, you will not find Lorenzo Semple Jr. anywhere mentioned. Original story from a novel by James Houston, screenplay by James Houston, adaptation by Martin Ransohoff—I mean holy shit, Martin Ransohoff, the guy's an A-list producer—followed by screenplay by Tom Rickman, for God's sake. Got an Oscar for *Coal Miner's Daughter* and should have got another for *Kansas City Bomber*. You can tell this was a production in trouble, particularly when you understand that Phil Kaufman was a gorgeous writer all on his own. And yet Lorenzo Semple Jr. is there. On the set in What the Fuck, Canada, or Inuit, Alaska, way north, punching up the script. I always loved that image: the writer like a baker punching up dough, bruising it, swelling it to the proportions the producer had in mind. And now Lorenzo is back, to regale us with tales of wimpy polar bears in the frozen north. They auditioned local polar bears—there was an essential scene, twelve-foot polar bear rears up, roars, claws, threatens the stranded whalers (Timothy Bottoms—bless his heart, nice Santa Barbara boy, wonderful in *Last Picture Show*), Warren Oates (long dead, long missed. My favorite actor in the world. You could watch a thought cross Warren Oates's face the same way you could a watch a furrow cross a dog's brow as a flung roast chicken passed overhead. Bless him. *Two Lane Blacktop* and *The Wild Bunch* live forever, because of Warren Oates.), and the underrated Louis Gossett Jr. Still alive, a pain on the set, I'm told; I'll be more reverential to him when he is not.

The local polar bears, according to Lorenzo, were not satisfactory. They could roar, they could claw, they could rear up, but not on cue, and when there was seal blubber or salmon present—part of the actor reward system—they couldn't concentrate at all and would only claw through the mess tent and chow down. And whack anyone who tried to interrupt. So, the trained polar bear, Jethro, is flown in from Thousand Oaks, California. Makeup problems, because the bear has a lot of blonde and green fur from his chlorinated pool in Thousand Oaks. Also, the bear has to wear sunglasses because he is not used to the ice-glare in this horrid part of the world. Also, he kind of doesn't like the cold and actually has stand-by assistants with down blankets and blow-dryers rushing toward him at the end of each scene. Jethro does satisfactorily complete his scene, rising, rearing, roaring, clawing at the sky, and then retires. It's two weeks before the plane comes back for Jethro, and in that time the crew learns that Jethro hates the local polar bears, will have nothing to do with them, and may in fact be gay, or at least is caught humping several (male) huskies, a stand-in walrus (who can tell), and two dead seals. His last days on the set are punctuated by his humping of Warren Oates's fur covered leg. Warren, according to Lorenzo, says, *Hell yes, bring on that lonely fella! I been there.*

We are collapsed with laughter at the end of this recitation, all except Jaime Rubin, who has a new gleam in his eye that poetry will never satisfy. He is particularly fascinated by the way that Lorenzo Semple Jr. *tells* his story.

Lorenzo Semple Jr. has one of the great performance tics in the history of neglected screenwriters. I haven't brought it in until now because it's an interruption—that's exactly what Lorenzo does. He's talking, mild but charismatic balding guy, and then he does this *thing*.

He's saying, "So Dino, he's explaining to me why we *havea* to makea this movie and he saysea"—and then there is this frozen moment where Lorenzo Semple Jr., I swear to God, has this out-of-body experience. He steps aside from himself, turns his head, and goes: *Ehhh!* Then, he returns to himself and says—"*Everabody likea the Big Monkey!*"

It's a tic, but not involuntary. It's not Tourette's, and I'm sure that there are many legal and medical reasons for this, but what strikes me is that this is a fabulous device. He punctuates his talk with the *ehhh!* But not at measured intervals. Sometimes, there are two-minute gaps—which build suspense. Sometimes the *ehhhs!* are only a few seconds apart: *So, this fucking giant polar bear, ehhhh!, he has issues with the local polar bears, ehhhh! He doesn't think they smell good, he doesn't like what they eat, he's used to McDonald's, sushi if he has to, ehhhh!*"

Jaime Rubin is riveted, and afterward he hangs out and

hangs out and hangs out, a half hour altogether so that he can be the last guy to talk to Lorenzo Semple Jr. And what he asks is, "What's with the *ehhhh!*?"

Lorenzo says, "Whaddya mean? Whaddya talking?" and Jaime, because he is a bright student and on his way to really understanding the business, asks, "So when you go into a meeting with these high-power guys, I mean directors and producers and guys who can throw up on tuxedoes and throw them away, how do you get their attention?"

And Lorenzo, understanding that he is not dealing with a total idiot, is gentle. "I had a roommate at Saint Paul's," he said. "British kid, Simon. I thought Simon was maybe the lamest, softest, most hopeless kid I ever met. He had this terrible stutter. He'd s-s-s-sssay-y-y-yy, I-I-I-I don-n-n-n't think I can-n-n-n, and I'd go back to what I was already doing. But then I watched him in class. The teachers were hyper-aware of his affliction and would always throw him a lob question, and Simon would say, 'I-I-I-I th-th-th-i-i-i-ink-nk...' and eventually he would come out with it, but what mattered was that we were all—*all*—entirely focused on Simon, until he got it out. And I had to spend half my junior year in the lobby because Simon hung a permanent towel on the doorknob. I mean, he had a waiting list of Sensitivoes dying to fuck him.

"When I finally got to England, I learned it was an upper-class affectation. A way of guaranteeing that people hung on every word. Can't work here, because we're more democratic and impatient and American, so I adapted. Nice meeting you, kid. We never had this conversation, and don't ever use my name as a reference. And don't ever use my schtick. I'll hear about it. Invent your own. Good luck. *Ehhhh!*"

Jaime, dazzled, tried to generate a screenwriting program at UC Irvine, terminally disappointing his poetry teachers who were sure that his proposed epic on Sephardim in Seattle would be an honorable failure. He quit after the first year and went to work as an intern on *Jeopardy*. A wise career choice. I was stupid and stayed, to work on that epic novel about swimmers, *Treading Water*. Guess what, swimmers swim; they don't fucking read.

So Jaime makes his adaptation on Lorenzo Semple's genius tic. Or he tries. He tries mock-Tourette's, which works pretty good until he runs up against a casting director whose kid actually had Tourette's, and she put the word out on Jaime big time. He never got onto the Warner's lot again. Eventually Jaime decided he would wing it and developed an involuntary gesture, a jerky lift of his elbow he called "the wing" that he used to punctuate his pitches. It looked a little like the move that Walter Brennan used in *The Real McCoys* combined with Jack Nicholson's waggle in *Easy Rider* whenever he took a drink from his flask, but Jaime didn't make the same "Nick-Nick" noises, and his move was a little more violent. The problem Jaime faced was twofold: One, a reputation for eccentricity works fine at the top-end, when anyone who can deliver a script that will generate twenty million worldwide is accorded lots of elbow room. Two, Jaime was not working the high end; he was trying this act on people like Roger Corman and Samuel Arkoff. Jaime got so wound up in a script pitch with Arkoff, a musical about the true talent in the family "Mrs. Mozart," that he whacked Arkoff's favorite designated secretary under the chin with an errant elbow. That pretty much ended Jaime's movie career, and television, while occasionally enriching, was not the place for him. If there is one thing that any serious television guy can sniff out, it's ambivalence. Jaime still loved good writing and purpose and thought serious work could be done. His models were from the late '50s and '60s, Alcoa Theatre, the US Steel hour. This was the '80s.

Jaime called it integrity; they smelled ambivalence. He'd make a script sale, he always had good ideas, but he never made it to staff; they preferred to rewrite him. He wasn't a team player.

Jaime has basically been retired since the mid-nineties, breakfast at the Farmers' Market, noon call to his agent, who hasn't sold anything since the mid-nineties, afternoons at Bowdler's, which are precious to him. Oscar and I get his jokes; Oscar and I get Jaime. Not many now do.

Jaime is dry. He looks sadly at his empty glass and then at Oscar. "Forgive me, mein herr. It shouldn't be your turn, but it is, because once again, our favorite Union Steward is not working. Surprise, surprise."

No surprise, really. That Union Business. My Principled days, my Firebrand days. Jaime can never leave it alone. Even now, I can barely talk about it. Unlike my apotheosis, which I knew when it happened, I hadn't a clue when I was poised above the abyss.

In the 1988 strike, I was a Watch Captain. I organized the pickets, scheduled meetings, and listened to endless grievances and gossip provided by my fellow writers-and-strikers. One of them, a staff writer (a disgruntled staff writer it turned out, a phrase that always makes me wonder what a gruntled staff writer would look like) on a top-ten adventure/comedy going into its sixth year (Terms of Settlement forbid the utterance of the name of this Network Cornucopia or the name of the Writer/Producer who developed the series). The staff writer, let's call her *Miss-Dis-Gruntled*, gave me to understand that her boss was a Shriker (a term I had invented for Shirking Strikers); he was continuing to work on scripts during the strike, breaking the most fundamental rule that applied to Union members. *Miss-Dis-Gruntled* presented me with copies of script revisions, dated post-strike, and tapes of what seemed to be phone conversations regarding shows that were currently being shot. I filed the complaint.

In response: Lava, bile, boiling-oil, burning-tar, hot-rocks, slime, ooze, napalm, cooties, and indelible stains were poured and catapulted on me by a well-coordinated team of publicists, reporters, Studio Flacks, and even Union Functionaries, who had clearly been waiting for my single, feeble flare.

The Writer/Producer insisted that all the script revisions and phone conversations had taken place before the strike and reminded the Strike Committee, that I, Dale Davis, had submitted three scripts for the well-known series, all of which had been turned down, without encouraging words. He didn't even have to remind them that he himself was the Horn-of-Plenty, for his network, for his production company, and for the eighty-plus people he employed.

Miss-Dis-Gruntled disappeared, meantime, and when she reappeared, it was with a production deal at an unrelated but sympathetic Network. She was well and truly gruntled, and her recollection now was that I had solicited complaints. The strike ended, and so did my career.

Within a year, my agent had dropped me, and my scripts— sent out by me, over the transom since I couldn't find a new agent—were returned unread. I tested this. I glued together script pages at random. None were ever separated. The scripts came back, unread, untouched. The same scripts, submitted to the same shows, by a friend who acted as a front, were returned, but with interest and the suggestion to try again. And two were sold. My friend, the front, took 10 percent on the first script, 50 percent on the second when he realized his risk.

I slid down the ladder a lot faster than I had climbed it. Within a year, I couldn't even find a reputable front. After two, I was teaching night classes in screenwriting at three community colleges. Not advanced classes, or intermediate, just beginning. Advanced and intermediate classes were reserved entirely for regular faculty, none of whom had any screen credits but had something more important: seniority and tenure.

• •

A DISTURBANCE IN THE FORCE. THE PADDED FRONT door cracks open, light streaks in and pins we mole people at our table; a slim figure in a trench coat over tights slips through, and the doorway bonks shut behind her. Jaime claws the air in horror. It is Alice Shortley, the owner of Bowdler's, an hour early from her yoga class. Jaime tries to be out of here before Alice arrives. One cannot express the terror that is felt by large, ineffective men in the presence of small, fierce women who know what they are doing. Alice has purpose. We do not have jobs that can be described, even if we were working. We are ungainly.

Alice tolerates eccentricity but not familiarity, and it is this memory that terrifies Jaime. Eight years ago, when Alice took over after her father's death, Jaime tried to greet her the first time she came through the door, with a toast, "To Alice! New owner of a misnamed-bar, Bowdler's. Your dad couldn't spell Baudelaire's, which was what he meant. Your Dad loved French poetry! To Alice. To Baudelaire's!"

It was eight in the evening. Good crowd. They raised their glasses, toasted: "To Alice! To Baudelaire's!"

Alice, in sweats, took a hard, nearsighted look at Jaime and his corner and turned to Kenny the Bartender and said, "Is that guy running a tab?" Kenny nodded. "Cut him off," Alice said. "Have him clear his tab, and tell him not to come back."

Jaime paid his tab, stayed away about two months, and then brazened days. He lives in mortal fear of Alice, who now ignores him. On this day, Jaime is tired of living in terror, and after clawing the sky, he addresses Alice. "Your Dad did want to call this place Baudelaire's. He was afraid no one would get it."

Alice is looking at receipts and doesn't look up, and then she does. "That fucking neon sign is a city-approved historical landmark," she says. "Bowdler's. Bowdler's is what we got. You want to lead the million-dollar campaign to change the name, be my guest."

Jaime claws the sky again. "I knew it. I knew it. I was fucking right."

"You're right," Alice says, packing paper-clipped stacks of bills, checks, receipts, and her account book into a gym bag. "You're always fucking right, and it's irritating. Keep it up, and you're going to get 86ed again." She zips the bag and is moving, bonks the door open, crack of white light freezing we mole people, and gone.

"Oh, God dammit," Jaime moans, "I've been Bowdlerized."

Oscar stirs a bit, sips at his creme de cacao. "Forget it, Jaime," Oscar says. Then he gives the perfect pause, just the way they did in *Chinatown*, and concludes, "It's Hollywoodski."

Jaime stands up, a fierce gesture. This is not Jaime standing up on his way to the bathroom. Jaime thrusts up, on his way to build the barricades. "I must make amends. I must sacrifice. It is a far, far better thing I do, than I have ever done before…" He lurches to the bar and grabs the jumbo lighter fluid can next to the cash register.

Oscar sways up, still seated, and blubbers, "SSSShanctu-aary!… Charles Laughton, goddamn great actor."

"You're mixing your movies, guys," Kenny says. "Put the lighter fluid back."

Jaime finds his mark, ten feet from the door, clear, and under the only pin spot in the place. Before Kenny can get up, Jaime turns and lays down a circular track of lighter fluid, turning once, twice, and then flicks and holds a lit match.

"Oh, fuck, Jaime," Kenny says, "Do you have to do this?"

"I must atone," Jaime says, "I must expiate the Bowdler's curse." Kenny holds his head; Jaime flicks a match and drops it.

"Johnny Cash," Oscar says, his great head lifting as Jaime is encircled by blue flames.

"Wrongo-Bongo," Jaime says to Oscar. The flames turn orange as they die back and Jaime lays another track, turning. "I'll give you a clue." The flames turn blue again. "Death by fire is a terrible thing." Jaime holds a hand against his brow as the metaphoric flames rise higher; the actual flames, a half inch high, are starting to shrink and yellow. "Send me back to God, from whom I came."

Oscar, for once, is stumped, and I step in as I get to do about once a year. "Ingrid Bergman in *Joan of Arc*, 1948, a good movie that tanked because Ingrid had run off with Roberto Rossellini. They had a bastard kid, and while all good Americans wanted to see Ingrid burned at the stake, they just couldn't believe her as a virgin."

As the flames die down and wink out, Kenny says, "Why do you have to be such an asshole?"

Jaime fehhs a hand at him, that disgusted but feeble downward wave only TV writers of a certain vintage know how to do. "Oyzhe, assholes. Whattya know from assholes? Assholes are like marriages. Everybody's got two."

Oscar stirs from his liquered slump. "Good line. I don't know that line. What movie is that from?" And Jaime says, with a lift and slump of his shoulders, "Unproduced script. *Ehhhh!* My life."

- TUTORIAL -

(2009)

TUTORIAL

(2009)

COMING OUT OF THE FREEWAY TUNNEL IN SANTA Monica is a transformation. Dark, subway-tiled, no radio reception, then, instantly a burst of music, blue sky, white sand, and the glory of the ocean across Pacific Coast Highway. I feel like an ancient Greek ascending from the underworld.

I am on my way to a Christian college in Malibu, a place I haven't been in over a year since my banishment. Under the terms of my non-disclosure agreement, I won't mention the name. Like a lot of cults, they are extremely litigious.

What I mostly remember about the place, aside from the incredible views—green lawn sloping down to the ocean across PCH—is the incredible dissonance of the parking lots. The shaded student lot was nestled close to the heart of campus. We adjuncts called it the Opera Lot, because like opera, Italian and German prevailed. The names of most cast members ended in *i*—Ferrari, Maserati, Lamborghini. The Wagnerian section ran toward custom Mercedes, after-market Porsches, Beemers for the non-working poor. Then there were the Unicorns, cars I couldn't name with doors that cantilevered out, pivoted and swung skyward with the pneumatic grace of a debutante after twelve years of cotillion training.

The adjunct faculty lot was a mile downslope, with shuttle-service so irregular we all developed healthy Christian hiking habits, which may have been the point. We ran toward pallid and paunchy. Our sunbaked cars ran toward oxidized Civics, Sentras, and Corollas, most bearing parking stickers for two or three community colleges. Mine may have been the only American car, a Saturn as ragged as the rest. We were Freeway Flyers, the true name residing behind adjunct professor. The most tattered among us bore bumper stickers—*Question Authority, Boycott Grapes*—dating to the decade when we still cared.

I was heading to Malibu for the first time in a year because one of my former students, Omar Saud Tayi, had won the annual campus screenwriting competition, the Veritas Lux Prize, $20,000 he didn't need, and a meeting with a William Morris agent, which no one needs.

Like every Saudi student I'd ever worked with, Omar claimed to be royal, but in his case it might have been true. He made sure he left no secular traces that might get him recalled to the homeland. He went by Omar, or Homer—"like Simpson" or sometimes "like Seempson" he'd tell his Christian fellow students—but his screenplay and social media pseudonym was Aladdin Elay, as in *ALadinLA.com*.

I'd had Omar/Homer/Aladdin for an introductory screenwriting class, and we'd hit it off. He couldn't write a lick, but he could talk really well, which is sometimes enough for a career in my biz, and he brought really good wines for our after-class discussions.

He started talking me up with his fellow students—probably the start of my downfall—calling attention to my IMDB credits and Writers Guild currency. This is almost always a mistake in academe, particularly when the head of the film program, also the dean of the arts—on sabbatical when I was hired—had mustered three credits on Christian television over thirty years before and then listed producer credits for twenty-nine years of student films on his C/V. As we say in the trade, Christian film-making is to filmmaking as military music is to music.

When I signed on to teach, I was required to sign a state-ment attesting to my belief in God, in Jesus Christ his only son, and my regular attendance at church services, not required to be *Church of Christ* but strongly suggested. With my screenwriting background, minor-league lies like these were as involuntary as breathing. I did list an ex-brother-in-law, who had bought a Uni-versal Life Minister's certificate, as my pastor.

Once Omar put the heat on me, even the dean had no prob-lem building a case. My ACLU membership (though lapsed for non-payment of dues) was a matter of public record, my Face-book friends skewed seriously Semitic, and my ex-brother-in-law, my pastor, denied me. I was declared a Secular Humanist.

My classes were canceled, my former students were coun-seled—"at great expense," I was told—in the letter that explained my potential liabilities should I be inclined to sue. Only Omar reached out and hired me, privately, to help with his screenplay. Months of hard work on someone's part—a collaboration much like those I'd previously experienced with the executive wing—produced Omar's award-winning screenplay, *Bang!*, a thriller with a threatened nuclear apocalypse and Middle Eastern am-bience.

I'm approaching Malibu. The pier is to my left, Christmas lights ringing the pilings, but I enjoy only a millisecond glance. The stoplight has blinked orange, and with only a quarter mile to the intersection, I have to start pumping the brakes. The problem has been explained to me many times. The brake pads are gone, the rotors are warped, and the master cylinder is going. I have my priorities. I paid for the new battery and starter. The important thing is to get to the meeting. You can figure out how to stop along the way, and once you are there, no one can see your car.

That's why, like a lot of writers, my phone is worth more than the car it rides in.

Each time I hit the brakes, the steering wheel kicks side to side and the pedal pulsates. I slow enough, with honking behind me, that the light is green when I reach it, and I slide on through and ease over, a mile up the road by the campus entrance.

The long and winding road up to campus central is once again marked by the signs that confused the hell out of me the first time I saw them. Just after the entrance is the first, a long rectangular sign with block lettering, "ONE WAY!" that makes no sense at all; at that point the road is four lanes wide, with grassy center medians, and cars and trucks are coming down in those opposite lanes. A partial explanation comes four hundred yards later with the second sign: "THE ONLY WAY!" Another quarter mile and three staggered signs give the final explanation: "ONE WAY!," "THE ONLY WAY," and then the payoff sign with gold-flecked highlights, "JESUS CHRIST—OUR SAV-IOR." The signage is provided by *Christian Splendor*, which is considered the cutting-edge evangelical club on campus. The signs appear and then vanish depending on administrative whim. Security and the relative sophisticates hate them; the more open-minded among the deans think it's youthful missionary fervor and ask the question that is raised in all campus debate: What would Jesus do?

I park discreetly at the lot closest to the faculty dining wing of the student center. At the information desk, I wait to ask directions to the Veritas Lux awards banquet. Chiseled into the marble wall in front of me is the school's affirmation statement. Number three on the list is the one they nailed me on: *That the educational process may not, with impunity, be divorced from the divine process.* As I said at the time, the school may believe in grace, but that does not extend to writing style. The clear-eyed young man who gives me my directions says, "Gosh. They've got you in the John the Baptist Room. This must be a big event for you."

I don't actually make it all the way to the Suite John B. In the hallway next to the kitchen's swing doors is an angry knot of old white guys and Omar, arguing and blocking the way of the laden waiters and waitresses trying to move food.

I recognize my nemesis, Dean Wayne Harolde. Dean Wayne is flushed to a raspberry hue usually reserved for the cheeks of Hummel figurines.

Omar has his hands out in full supplication. "But he's my guest," Omar pleads. "I invited him!" Every time one of Omar's hands moves, Dean Wayne flinches slightly. Then he spots me. He raises an arm and points at me, finger quivering like a compass needle settling on Vile North. "That man is not allowed on this campus!" Omar claps a hand on top of his head. "You can't come in here," Dean Wayne quavers.

I wave to Omar, who looks like the hand is the only thing keeping his head from exploding, then to the dean, and try the theological option, "Ummm ... Hate the sin, forgive the sinner?"

Dean Wayne turns to his hench-boys. "Go get security!" They back away and then jog off, one turning to smile at me with delight as they slip out the back door.

Dean Wayne glares. "Did you park in the visitors' lot?"

I hold out my parking ticket. "Do you think I could get validated?" That turns the dean theological.

"We're not going to validate you. We're not going to validate you!"

That stings. "You were my last hope."

Dean Wayne starts to back away, feeling behind him for the kitchen door. When he feels the swinging door give, he jabs a finger at me. "We'll have you towed. We'll have you towed." He butts open the door and pivots to the kitchen. As the door swings back and forth in diminishing arcs, a satisfactory crash emerges from somewhere in the depths—glasses, dishes, maybe even crockery.

"Well," I tell Omar, "that went about as well as can be expected. Can I borrow ten bucks for parking?"

Omar shifts gears in a way that makes me think there may be diplomats in his family. "So, they wouldn't let you come to the awards luncheon. So what? We're going to lunch, Buddy. Just you and me."

The networking conciliator in me wants him to cover his ass. "Don't do it, Omar. This is your day; you should enjoy it. They're going to say nice things about you. Don't piss them off."

"Don't worry about it. I got it covered. I already got the check. Where do you want to go?"

Where do I want to go? It's Malibu—there's only one answer. "Malibu Seafood."

"Cool," Omar says. "Find a parking spot down by the nursery. Call me when you're there. I'll pick you up in ten." Kindness on Omar's part, he wants me parked in the shade. Also, discretion: It's far enough from campus he probably won't be seen picking up a shabby old guy driving a car that does not signify. We're outside now, and I spot a doughnut of security guards rolling toward the back door of the building. Guns are not drawn, but they are present. I head for the parking lot as Omar reaches for his wallet. "Kidding about the parking," I say. "It was the perfect scene-ender."

In ten minutes, I make the call from Consentino's Nursery. Ten minutes later I watch a gleaming red sculpture ascend the hill and glide to a stop like honey pooling. Omar is too cool for school. Omar is so cool he has removed the prancing horse insignias from his Ferrari—which confuses the shit out of most of Malibu. "I don't want to be a cliché," he explained.

The door swings wide, displaying tan leather so supple I must assume it comes from unborn calves. Behind me, I can feel my

Saturn shrink. "Get in, Buddy," Omar says. "It's time to cele-brate."

"Omar, you shouldn't have pissed off the dean." Distilled wisdom from my own experience. I try.

"Don't worry," says Omar. "I know you can't be happy, but don't worry. I will explain it all to you. Get in."

I lower myself into the tan lap of luxury. The door closes with a precise click, the same sound, I imagine, as that of a bank vault in Zurich. Two seconds later, before I can find my seatbelt, Omar punches it. In three seconds, we are past sixty miles an hour and I realize I don't need a seatbelt. I am pressed back so hard in the seat I think of the giant octopus movie I once rewrote. Omar shifts to second, and within ten seconds I've become the total cliché: old white guy in a red Ferrari, hitting a downhill ninety per, while scanning the sand and water ahead. The turistas we pass crane their heads to see what famous, fabulous creatures might be inside God's red capsule. It raises a smile, and Omar, looking over, smiles as well and slaps my shoulder. "Your day too!"

He really is a nice kid. You usually have that double-edged thing with the really rich: They expect you to listen intently when they talk; they've been raised on that. But they've also learned that attention might be because of the money, which makes them wary, and you get watched carefully in those one-sided conversations. They are prepared for betrayal and ready to turn on a dime. Omar doesn't have so much of that. He actually listens. And he's genuinely funny. The whole "Buddy" thing is his invention, based on Iranian née Persian stereotypes from the '90s. I've watched him deal with his Christian counterparts. The whole "Omar, like Homer, like Seempson" is another invention. Makes them comfortable, even though they have no idea who he is. Or that he can pronounce Simpson better than most English actors.

Corral Canyon Beach on our left, we ease up the steep drive-way of Malibu Seafood market. My legendary parking luck is in play. A Turista van backs out of a parking slot, right in front of the building. Omar accepts this as his due, but my version is this: When I was born, I was asked, You wanna be the Messiah? And I said, What else you got? They said, Parking Luck? And I said, yeah, I'll take that one. And it is true. I can arrive at the Vista Theater on Sunset, famous for its lack of parking, ten minutes before the special screening of *Double Indemnity*, and Barbara Stanwyck's chauffeur will vacate my spot next to the theater.

Parking luck does not, however, extend to gracefulness. The Ferrari is so low that when I open my door and lean out to swing it wide, I am looking at pebbled asphalt eight inches from my nose. I trust that everyone is watching Omar emerge on the driver side and adjust his plumage, so I make my crablike slide, roll, gather, and stand. Like, *What?* I join Omar as we join the line. He lets me go first.

Malibu Seafood is the one egalitarian oasis in Malibu. Doesn't matter who you are or what you want to spend, you start at the end of the line.

The sunburned tourist ahead of me, sporting an Arizona State Sun Devils hat, says, "Nice car." He's actually addressing Omar, but I take charge. "Thanks. It's a rental. Me and the driver"—I chuck my head toward Omar—"are here to scatter my wife's ashes. She always wanted to see Malibu." I turn away on that conversation-ender and watch Omar assemble his insulted but still-hoping-for-a-tip chauffeur face.

The Sun Devil conveys the news to his family. The line stirs. I am regarded reverently by four pink balloon animals, swollen by sun. In Arizona, I assume, they spend their days in shade and AC. Their eyes fall as I cover my face with my palms. Behind me, I can hear Omar choking back laughter. "Fucking Dale," escapes him.

The line is short, for a Friday. We're at the door in ten, after refusing the Zonies' offer to move ahead of them.

Inside, the refrigerated case displays row after row of shining, bright-eyed fish on chipped ice—blue-fleshed lingcod, Petrale sole, sanddabs, red snapper. Glossy piles of shrimp, spot prawns, mounds of black mussels, oysters, and clams. The joint is owned by commercial fishermen, and their bounty is impeccable. Not a whiff of fishiness.

I have a history here. It was a weekly treat when I was teaching at the Christian college. Long before that, whenever business took me coastal, I'd insist on Malibu Seafood as the meet-place.

I once ran into Jesse Gallo here, ten years after my failed directorial debut with *Head-In-Bag*. Jesse hadn't become what I'd hoped, the next Warren Oates. Instead, he'd become the next Jan-Michael Vincent, but he'd done well enough as the lead in money-laundering thrillers shot in Eastern Europe and Dubai to afford a cottage on the landlocked side of Point Dume.

I'd waved at him, across the patio, and he came over. The healthy tan at a distance was cracked sandpaper up close, and even dark glasses couldn't hide the spinning pinwheels behind them. We exchanged the usual—"long time no see," et cetera—but by the time he'd segued to "nice to see you again," I understood he had no idea who I was or had once been. Maybe it was wear and tear on my end as well.

The last bit of business I'd done here was about a year later, when my last agent bought me lunch and fired me. Ben Sturgis was a genuinely good dude, an old-line lefty, once a member of the Lincoln Brigade, and I think it broke his heart to fire me, but he didn't have a choice. His boutique agency had been swallowed whole by CAA, and one of their prime clients was the showrunner and strike-breaker who had given me the taint. Scab-boy made a point of snipping my last safety net.

Over day-boat scallops and fries, which Ben wouldn't eat, he lowered the blade. The bottom line, Ben said, was that either I went, or we both did. At seventy-three, with three wives' worth of alimony and four kids in college, he had no choice.

I absorbed the news and about half of Ben's fries. Ben left in tears. I actually took his scallops home, which shows how distracted I was. Nothing sadder than leftover seafood in a bachelor refrigerator, where it will sit for months. The next day I sold the Mercedes and bought the Saturn, new.

We've reached the counter, and Jeff, one of the owners, remembers me. "Good timing, Dale. Tom was in this morning." Tom is Tom Moore, a locally famous diver in his eighties who specializes in Pacific lobster. According to local legend, Tom once bit a shark that had bothered him. I look in the live case; a half-dozen of the spiny beauties are piled up in the corner. Food of the gods.

"Grande or chico?" Jeff asks. "Chico," I answer. "Always." My ideal is about a pound and a quarter. I've had this argument with East Coast boasters for years, who think Maine lobster is the pinnacle. It is not. The best lobster in the world comes from the Pacific coastline. Spiny lobsters, no claws, tails twice the size of East Coast ocean cockroaches. The problem is that they don't travel well. Not as hardy as the cucarachas, they fade from the day they are caught. But cooked the day they are caught, they are the world's most delicately flavored crustacean. Right up there with abalone on any gustatory bucket list.

"Chico and fries," I tell Jeff, "and a bowl of chowder." Omar is lobstered out this week. Visiting relatives have taken him repeatedly to Providence, Jonathan Gold's top-ranked restaurant three years running. He wants fish tacos, with a twist. "Do you have any grouper today?"

"White sea bass," Jeff says, "but only filets, in the market." Omar buys a three-pound filet, donates two pounds of it to Jeff, happy to spend about twenty bucks each for four fish tacos. Omar flashes cash, Jeff hands us our buzzer, and Omar makes me accompany him to the Ferrari. He pops the trunk, in front on this mid-engined beast, and reveals the ultimate party car. Nearly filling the sloping space is a custom refrigerator, picnic hamper with accoutrements, and wine cellar. Omar gathers ice, two Riedel crystal wine glasses, and a leather-covered ice bucket, which looks like the same tan leather as the upholstery but embossed with the only remaining prancing horse on the car. He opens the wine cellar, which requires a key, selects two bottles, and plunges them into the ice.

We sit down at our prime, shaded cement table, just vacated by a Latino family who seemed to have been waiting for us. Either my parking luck again or a surreptitious tip from Omar.

Omar twirls one of the bottles in the ice water, lifts it, cuts the foil with the folding blade of what seems to be a platinum-plated corkscrew. Three precise, full twists of the corkscrew and Omar hoists the cork, as gracefully as any sommelier I've seen. He smells the cork and smiles, then pours. I study the bottle when he sets it down on the table. It's not a Chateau I know, Domaine des Comtes Lafon Montrachet, so I whip out my phone and take its photo. At home I will learn that what I guzzled that afternoon was the equivalent of what I was paid to teach at that Christian college.

Omar raises his glass in a toast. "To Dale and Omar," he says. "What a team!" The cynic in me would think, a team requires a coach and players. Fair enough. Omar played. He played at writing. He absorbed enough of the evil bible—McKee's *Story Structure*, beloved of Suits and all those looking for a system that rids the biz of bothersome writers—to know he needed plot points. Omar had two solutions and two only: another car chase, another shoot-out. The first version of his script that I read contained nine shoot-outs and seven car chases. It also had a ticking nuclear bomb in a Versace purse. I suggested a suitcase might be the more appropriate size. Omar accepted the suggestion. "Louis Vuitton, right?"

My cynical reverie is interrupted by the first sip of wine. My eyes slowly shut, involuntarily, reverently, and a tear nearly squeezes out. "Omar. This wine is amazing."

"Sometimes," Omar says, "you just have to do things right."

The buzzer vibrates and blinks on the table between us, and Omar goes to collect our food. I won't leave the table; this is a wine that needs to be guarded.

The wine is even better with food. The French are so much better at that than our oaked, drink-alone wines. The lobster is sublime, a taste I hope to recall on my deathbed, so I can die smiling. It almost doesn't need the clarified butter or lemon.

Neither of us says a word; this food demands our full attention. The tacos look great as well, Ensenada style, battered with cabbage and crema. Omar opens the second bottle, probably a step down, but anything but Château d'Yquem would be. I finish the fries, dipping them in tartar sauce.

The sun has reached just the right angle, and the ocean is now in full sparkle. A pod of dolphins, less than a quarter mile from the beach, is chasing a school of bait fish into the shallows, followed by gulls and pelicans who drop like stones into the water. Hang gliders swirl around the point, riding the thermals in long spirals, and a long white yacht that looks like a sparkling recumbent hotel glides by close to the horizon. California dreaming. I raise my glass again. "I wonder what the poor people are doing."

Omar goes to get our espressos and some special biscotti from the Ferrari larder.

Time to talk. "Omar, my son, this was a lovely lunch, but you have now thoroughly pissed off Dean Wayne by skipping out on his luncheon. How are you going to make that man happy again?"

Omar flicks a hand as expressively as an unworried Italian conveying a trainload of nonchalance. "No problems." He pats his pocket. "I got the check."

"Yeah, but the man can hurt your career. You need him for letters of recommendation when you apply for film school. And what about your meeting with the agent?"

"That guy? They gave him a glass of wine before lunch, and he took a nap on the table. Know what he worked in? Radio."

"Okay, but you still need the dean on your side. Eyes on the prize. He'll help you get into film school. You're still planning on film school?"

"I don't know, Dude," Omar says. "Since I got the Veritas Lux Prize, things are changing. But if I want film school, I got the dean handled." Omar starts to grin. "The dean has needs."

Oh Jesús, I'm thinking, why are Christian schools the worst. I look at him. "Omar? Really?"

His grin widens. "Maybe *needs* is too strong a word. The dean has desires, he has ambitions. Waynie's been working on a script, set in the Crusades. The pitch he made was, he's got the Christians covered. He thinks I might be good at the Moorish side. Add authenticity."

Ooh, I think, the putz has a few more smarts than I credited him with. A note of authenticity, and, with Omar's involvement, possible financing. I study Omar. "You know why he's asking, right?"

"I know," Omar says. "He thinks I'll talk to my Uncle Ali, and Ali will give him his carrot. He's wrong. I hold the carrot. I just haven't decided what the stick is. And besides, his script is terrible. Really terrible. I could never fix it."

Terrible, I think. Omar now recognizes terrible writing when he sees it. Except his own. My job is done here. He's on his way to Producerhood.

Omar is feeling good, almost jaunty. I can remember that confidence. I wonder if my own was as unfounded. Omar expounds, "So. I haven't decided about film school. I may not need it. The Veritas Lux is kind of a big deal. Some agents have been in touch, and producers, who want to see more of my work."

More of my work, I'm thinking. Would that be the one about the killer whales who start coming ashore for easy midnight snacks, or the remake of *Cars*, where it turns out the real problem is gasoline addiction, and some cars will kill to get it.

Making them killer whales was actually my idea. Omar had written them as sharks, hadn't really thought through the whole gill thing.

"I'm thinking I'm going to enter some more contests and see what happens. I mean, I did win the Veritas Lux. Why shouldn't I win some others?"

Something in this conversation snags in my memory, and when I finally realize what Omar reminded me of, I start to laugh. Omar is prepared to be offended. "What's funny?"

"It's not you. But you just nailed one of the important plot points from one of my favorite novellas, *Rameau's Nephew* by Denis Diderot." Omar is baffled. I really don't want to step in any deeper here, so I say, "It's too hard to explain. I'll send you the book, and then you'll understand."

The sun is starting to lower, shorter days in December, even in Malibu. Time to go. Omar drives me back to my Saturn. As we park beside my ride, two thoughts. Thinking back to the morning, coming out of that tunnel, I compared myself to an ancient Greek, emerging from the underworld. So wrong. If I was an old Greek, I'd be driving a Kronos. I'm an old Roman. The second thought is that the Saturn has a lot more dents and scratches than I remember.

I lift myself out of the tan womb, and Omar gets out as well. At my door he hands across a very nice Margaux and an envelope.

In the envelope is a check. Two thousand dollars. "Ten percent, Buddy!" I'm touched. It means new brakes. It means I will make rent. It reminds me I'll face the same dilemma next month.

"Thank you, Omar. This is great. Maybe we should get started on some of your other scripts, for those other contests."

Omar looks down. When he looks up, those beautiful, buttery brown eyes are filled with sadness, or at least regret. "That's the other thing, Dale. Since the Veritas Lux happened, a bunch of really good writers have gotten in touch with me." He names some names. Their credits are much more recent, and they don't have my taint. The only thing we share is the Hollywood disease. We are not new. We are aging out.

I knew this would happen. It's an over-and-over thing. I just didn't think it would be this soon.

We shake hands, formally. "I will send you that book." Omar roars off. When I slide into Ion Boy, Saturn's given name, I pat the seat beside me, and when he starts, first twist of the key, I pat the sun-cracked dash. I may be forgiven.

Driving home against a stunning sunset, I'm trapped by my own metaphor. Entering the tunnel is entering the underworld and Charon's ferry stops in Culver City. It ain't Hades, but it is Culver City.

Rameau's Nephew was a book I remembered from a course on utopian fiction taught by a delightfully focused historian, Jonathan Beecher, whose expertise was cranky French socialists. Rameau was a famous French composer when the novella was written in the 1750s. It wasn't published in Diderot's lifetime. He'd already been jailed for his Encyclopedia and knew this book would offend even some of his allies. The book is a dialogue between Diderot and Rameau's nephew, a contradictory ne'er-do-well who would like to be famous, or at least rich, but is appalled by the prerequisites: hard work, talent. He imagines a better world in which he discovers some of his famous uncle's unknown compositions, after the old man has died, and publishes them as his own. And then, he addresses himself, now the new Rameau, "Rameau, you'd love to have composed those two pieces. And, of course, if you'd done those two, surely you could have done two others. And when you'd composed a certain number, people would play and sing you all over the place. When you walked along, you could hold your head high. Others would point you out. They'd say, 'There's the man who wrote those lovely gavottes.'"

I kept my word and sent Omar a copy of the book. About two months later I got a long text.

Hey dale, Omar here, remember me? I really liked that Rameau's Nephew thing you sent. I couldn't really read it, but I got a grad student to give me notes. I think it will make a great script. Gonna make a couple changes. I'm making him Rambo's Nephew and I'm putting in a time-travel twist. The guy doesn't wait for his Uncle to give him stuff. He goes to the future and grabs it. So that means two things. Rambo's nephew—I'm going to call him Xander Rambo—gets all the credit, and in the future the old Rambo guy looks bogus for trying to take credit from Xander. Cool huh? I also think I might make him an inventor instead of a musician. What do you think?

What do I think? I think Omar is well on his way.

– "INDIVIDUAL MEDLEY" –

A STORY BY DALE DAVIS

(1981)

INDIVIDUAL

MEDLEY

A STORY BY DALE DAVIS

(1991)

"INDIVIDUAL MEDLEY"

A STORY BY DALE DAVIS

(1981)

O N THE HILLSIDE WEST OF THE SWIMMING POOL, men with shovels followed the line of the fire, turning dirt onto glowing patches. Above them, on the ridge, a bulldozer clanked and roared as it cut a gap. The fire burned slowly through the dampened yellow grass, flaring only when a bush caught. Ashes lifted and broke apart, drifting down the hill. Ash rolled and scudded through the blackened stubble, across the green of the practice football field, wafting up to the chain-link fence surrounding the pool where it fluttered and broke on the wire.

Entering the pool enclosure, passing between gray bleachers, John Goodwin held his towel tightly against his side and dug into his jeans pocket for the dollar. The young girl who took the money sat cross-legged on a stack of kickboards, braiding her hair as she read the paperback held open between her feet. Holding the braid in place, she took the bill with her free hand and slipped it into the envelope beside her. John was looking out, across the pool and up the slope. A bright chartreuse pickup truck was bouncing through the smoke toward the fire crew. "It's a controlled burn," the girl said. "They started it this afternoon when school let out."

She handed him a clipboard with a pen tied to it, and John signed on a numbered line beneath a long paragraph, acknowledging that he would not hold the local school district or the State of California responsible for anything that happened to him in the pool.

"Did they say how long it would go on?"

She was reading his name. "What?" She looked up. "I guess until it burns out. Nobody said."

There were two other lap swimmers. John tossed his towel down behind the fifth lane. He stepped out of his sandals and unbuttoned his Levi's. Standing on one leg, he tugged at the other cuff and watched the lines of pale blue floats that divided the pool bob and turn. He listened to the slap of hands on the water and the soughing wash of the gutters. The odor of the fire was stronger here; he smelled the smoke on his sweater as he pulled it over his head.

John dabbed a foot in the water. It was warmer than the air, which was cooling rapidly as the sun lowered. He bent and dipped a hand in the water, splashed his legs, and rose, cupping another handful, which he tossed on his chest and rubbed on his shoulders. He dipped again, put his hands over his head, spread the fingers, and watched the water drip down past his eyes.

It was the oldest set of gestures he knew—the soothing ritual of a seven-year-old racer preparing to climb onto the starting block. His toes gripped the coping, his calves flexed, and his knees bent. He shook his hands out, looked down the lane, and breathed deeper and deeper. Hanging on the side fence was a large lap clock. John watched the sweep hand and sucked air explosively as it ascended.

He bent deeper and swung his arms back until he was coiled. The sweep hand edged twelve. His arms whipped around in a full arc, and he sprang. He was flat out over the water, trying to

hollow. On a good racing dive, he remembered, you should feel
like a cup. Descending, hands and feet should touch first. His
head was too low, and he plunged.

The water was a familiar shock, surrounding him like a cool,
cloudy gas. He knew he'd gone too deep on the dive to recover.
He relaxed, giving in to the gliding descent. One hand grazed
the bottom. He swept his arms back and frog-kicked and continued into an easy breaststroke that brought him to the surface
after half a lap. At the wall, he pulled into a curl and kicked off
into a backstroke. He watched his feet break water, kept his legs
straight, and concentrated on his arm pull. The line of red and
yellow plastic pennants, five yards from the end, came into view.
He stroked twice more and floated in to touch the wall.

It was Thursday. He'd come to swim every night that week,
the third week in a row. Each of those evenings he'd been surprised to find himself there and on time.

On the first night, after barely finishing a ten-lap set (he'd
almost walked the last yards), he'd been leaning against the wall,
stomach churning, gasping, when the swimmer in the next lane,
a bearded young man, also resting, looked over, nodded cheer-
fully, and said, "It feels good though, doesn't it?"

"Feels awful," John had said. He'd turned and folded his
arms on the edge of the pool and put his head down on them.
"Maybe it will get better. It's been fifteen years since I did any
real swimming."

The young man, who was tilting his head to one side and wig-
gling a finger in his ear, said, "Oh yeah? What were you doing?"

John reached behind the starting block and found his goggles. It was closer to twenty years since he'd swum competitively.
Goggles were one change in that time, a sensible one, but he
wasn't comfortable with them yet. The strap was always caught
and pulling in his hair. Water seeped in under the lenses unless
he pressed them down hard, and then they sealed so tight he

felt fish-eyed. The bubbled lenses were green. He hated the way they must look on him. The alternatives, as he'd learned the first few nights, were stinging eyes that remained a rabbity pink the next day, blurred vision underwater, and trouble with the lights when he drove home, although that part was beautiful: Colored nimbuses surrounded the lights, blue at center, radiating out to green and red, with lines, spoked like the lines of a pupil. He couldn't remember that his eyes had ever burned like that before, and he'd been in the water two to three hours a day, then. He assumed they were using more or harsher chemicals.

It was nearly dark. The line of the fire, two-thirds of the way up the hill now, was getting clearer. The bulldozer had stopped for the moment, and he could hear a light, rolling crackle of the burning grasses and shrubs. The fire crew were only visible when a flame spurted near them.

John adjusted his goggles and pushed off from the side. After a fast freestyle set, ten laps, he switched to breaststroke. It was a graceful stroke and established a rhythm. When he switched back to freestyle again, this rhythm would remain. His stroke would be even, his kick measured. These smooth, meditative laps had become the pursuit of the evening.

He'd started working out for other reasons. He'd wanted to redistribute a few pounds, and an article on quitting cigarettes had suggested that the discipline of exercise would ease the trauma. In the first few nights he'd had to concentrate on keeping himself afloat and counting laps. Once he had gained some endurance, the laps began to slip by with less effort, and he regarded the sessions differently, as a time in his day to think or dream.

John watched his arms pulling through, the air bubbles streaming back between his fingers. His stroke and kick were steady, his breathing economical. The laps began to slide by.

A letter had come from his mother. He had mentioned, in his

own letter, that he was swimming regularly. A clipping accompanied her letter. It wasn't really a clipping. It was a Xerox copy of a clipping, of a year-old story printed in his hometown newspaper. The story was about a summer league swim meet. Circled was a paragraph concerned with one race, the boys' eleven-to-twelve-year-old fifty-meter backstroke. The race had been won by a boy named Jerry Armendariz, in a new Southern Section record time. The sportswriter noted that it had been the oldest surviving record in the section, set eighteen years before by local swimmer John Goodwin. He'd smiled, reading it, thinking about how odd it was to be described as a "local swimmer." The clipping brought back a lot. He'd broken the old record by nearly two seconds, an impressive margin in a sport that recorded times by the hundredth part of a second. It had impressed a lot of people, including the sportswriter who had been there that night and who had devoted half a page to John.

. . . .

HE REMEMBERED THE NIGHT IN FRAGMENTS— smells, sensations, visions—that surfaced easily and always with pleasure. Verdugo Pool looked like an aqua keyhole from above, a long rectangle with two half-circle shallow areas at one end. The long building housing the office and locker rooms looked like a foreign legion desert fort—adobe-colored, with turrets and a notched roofline. There was a picnic area beyond one of the pool's side fences, wooden tables under an arbor. His family had a light dinner there, cold chicken and salad, before the meet. The arbor was roofed with dry palm fronds that rustled, always, and clattered in a wind. It was late August, the kind of night that makes tourists move to Southern California. The air was fresh, carrying the dusty fragrance of the manzanita down from the hillside and the light, sweet scent of the pittosporum hedge surrounding the pool. He remembered sitting on the sand-colored deck with his team, all of them waiting on neatly laid-out towels as their coach called their names and told them their events.

He could not remember the start of his race or the other swimmers. What came back was the feel of his body in the water. One arm lifted as the other descended, and his stroke was so strong that he felt he was riding up, almost out of the water. He felt the water surge over his body at each pull, like a current or electrical field; he felt the hairs moving on his arms and legs. He remembered touching the wall, fingers stretched perfectly at the end of a stroke, and then there was a beginning glow as the other swimmers churned in, and he finally sensed how far ahead of them he had been.

He was sitting with his family in the top row of the bleachers when the record was announced over the loudspeaker. The time drew whistles and gasps. His mother hugged him, and his father and sisters applauded. The applause descended the bleachers. People in the bottom rows stood up and turned toward him. He sat up straighter, beneath the blanket wrapped around him, smiled, and nodded shyly.

It was his last record. The next year, in May, just before the outdoor season, he broke his collarbone, landing wrong in the first attempt at a pole vault. When he finally returned to practice, he found his stroke had changed. He wallowed. His coach explained that a collarbone or shoulder injury would do that; he would have to alter his stroke.

At the end of that summer, a coach who had once headed the team at a rival YMCA phoned to invite John to join an AAU program. He was limiting the team to ten swimmers. "You'll be groomed," he said, "for the Olympics." John told him about the shoulder and explained that he'd hardly swum at all that year.

There was a silence. Finally, the man said, "Then you've definitely retired."

John said, "What?"

His older sister, who had answered the phone and remained, looked at him questioningly. The coach said it again, and this time John couldn't decide whether it was a statement or a question, but he answered, "Yes," in a voice that made his sister look at him again. "Yes. I guess I am."

. . . .

IN THE DARK, THE BULLDOZER GAVE A RATTLING BELlow, idled down, then roared again. It sounded like it was straining against something so heavy it had to rest between shoves.

John pushed off, beginning his forty-first lap. He sprinted the first lap, concentrating on the line on the bottom of the pool and then the black cross on the side that helped him gauge the turn. Two or three more laps and he would settle into a more reflective pace.

He'd taken the clipping to work and left it in his top desk drawer. He finally covered it with a sheet of paper. No one had caught him reading it, but he was embarrassed by his fascination. At one time his name had appeared in newspapers regularly, and he hadn't thought anything about it. What worried him about his fascination with the article was the possibility that it might be the last time his name would appear in print except the public notices section of the classifieds. It had appeared there twice that year and would be appearing again, in that curious column of ads that began: No longer responsible for any debts but my own. He had been amazed at the number of people he knew who read that section of the paper. A few brought it up, apologized, commiserated. There were more who hadn't said anything; he recorded the speculative looks and noted those who no longer asked after his wife.

The friends who had talked to him seemed shaken, and he could understand it. The marriage had always appeared solid. One friend, who had expected his own marriage would come apart long before theirs, told him: "You and Ellen got along. I never saw you guys fight. Not once." They had, of course, but never in public, and even privately their fights had consisted more of silences than of screaming. Right to the end, it was amazing how considerate they were of each other.

He had been calm that last day. Ellen had gone up the street to wait at a neighbor's house. The boys sat solemnly on the couch, hands carefully clasped in their laps. Todd, seven years old, had looked closely at his brother to see how he should fold his hands. Every time J.J. shifted, Todd leaned forward to look at him. At first, they sat upright, fingers laced, then, as they slumped, their hands went between their thighs, and they pressed their legs together.

John, sitting across from them, watched their faces. He felt they knew what was coming. They seemed braced. He told them he and their mother were separating, and their small, formal faces relaxed. They knew that word, "separating." More than half their classmates at Horace Mann Elementary were children of what the school referred to as single-parent families.

The boys only cried once, when he mentioned moving, and as soon as they understood they weren't moving, and that John wasn't taking either of the dogs with him, it was all right. They asked exactly what John was taking with him—what furniture, which car—and he began to realize that they had clear opinions of what was his, what was Ellen's, and what was theirs.

When he kissed them goodbye, he told them they would see him that weekend. He gave them both small cards with his new phone number, explaining that they should call any time, even if they only wanted to say goodnight. He stood on the porch and watched them walk down the street to the neighbors'. Todd kept looking at his card. J.J. took his hand as they crossed the street, and Todd looked up at him with mild curiosity.

· ·

THE FIRE ON THE HILL WAS OUT. THE BULLDOZER had completed the cut and chugged back over the ridge to its trailer. The truck and trailer had ground away moments before. Looking across the mist rising from the pool, John could see the fire crew walking back down the black hill. The moon was in front of them, low and bright. He could see them clearly, shovels over their shoulders as they walked, well apart, looking down. At the bottom, they moved together and clumped around the pickup truck. The shovels clattered into the bed. One of them laughed, and cigarettes were lit.

He floated on his back, resting. He had finished the eighty laps with a burst. His legs sank, and he stood. He raised his goggles and took them off, twisting his head to free the strap. Tossing the goggles onto the deck, he turned, rubbing his eyes, and looked at the clock. He was almost ten minutes ahead of his regular schedule. John felt his calves and rolled his shoulders. Everything was loose, not even the beginnings of a cramp, and he felt strong. He decided to swim another set, ten more laps.

The surface of the pool was glassy. Steam rose, collected, and drifted a foot above the surface. All the other swimmers were gone. The calm, shining corridor of water stretched ahead of him between the lane ropes. He pinched his nostrils, blew out, and sniffed. The smell of smoke and bleach was almost heady.

John pushed off. He started slowly, breaststroke. Ninety laps would be a new record. The water rippled away from him, small roiling furrows from each stroke and kick that smoothed before even reaching another lane. The pool had good gutters. He thought about Ellen on the last day. She had been so calm, so reasonable. It was almost insulting.

Without goggles, the water blurred around him. He was swimming a lap underwater—"lungbusters" his coach used to call them—to see if he could still do it. He strained and yet it was so quiet, and the lights were so odd—three plasticine bubbles on each side radiating yellow wavering rays and halos, like streetlamps on a submarine alley. He almost came up short. The last few strokes were on the surface and frantic. When he touched the wall, his head whipped back, and he gasped.

He had nearly blacked out during those last few strokes. The water was blurred, the light wavering, but what he saw in those last strokes was sharp-edged and clear. And familiar. He had seen both visions enough times, awake and dreaming, that much of the strangeness was gone from them: Himself at twelve on that August night, dripping, his hair wild, on the top step of the award stand; and then, like a hand shoved into his face and pulled back, so it came into focus moving away, Ellen's mask. It was her face at the moment he'd told her he was leaving, the one time her calm had broken.

Until that moment, Ellen's round, freckled, pretty face had only been bleak. When he said the words, she gasped. Her face ran together and then cracked; he'd thought about it a lot and that was what happened; her face cracked, fracturing in successive waves—astonishment, realization, certainty, and then absolute terror. The look of fear split it open. He had never seen fear like that in another person. Some part of him shriveled enough to let him register it almost dispassionately; it was like squinting when the light is too strong. It was the face in dreams and movies that smacks against the porthole or windshield, holds for an instant, then slips, drops away. Except that it remains.

Five more laps. Still gasping, swimming on the surface with

his head up, he continued. At the end of the lap, he was in stroke again. He swam one more lap of breaststroke, gathering strength and rhythm, feeling it build as he humped toward the wall. He turned so fast he was kicking into his wake. His first six strokes were without breath and by the sixth, as he turned to breathe under his arm, he felt he was almost above water. It was so smooth. His arms drove and he pulled through, and he was riding his kick. His body felt smooth, stretched to a fine tension, and he was beyond thought, no longer counting laps or planning the approach on turns. Blurring. Feeling the water rush over him. Pushing off the wall before he realized that he'd whipped down for the turn. The water surged through his hair.

On the last lap he began to tire but it was all right. He short-ened his stroke, willed his kick faster, and crashed through the water. All rhythm was gone, but he moved, chopping, rolling, to the wall. His hand smashed against the gutter, and he sank.

Hollowing his body, extending his arms and legs, he floated upward. He felt like an egg; his arms and legs felt tiny. He floated face down, his eyes closed, rocking gently in the remains of his wake. There was a light, pleasurable pressure at the back of his skull. Then his hand began to ache. He rolled over, his breath bubbling out, and wheezed and gasped as he tried to draw air. He wasn't just tired; he was weak. When he tried to stand, he was unable. He could hear and feel his heart thud on every breath, in and out, with a small catch each time. He massaged his hand. The moon was directly overhead. He had to tip back to see it. The moon bobbed as he slowly stirred his arms and legs until he was floating easily on the surface. His breathing became more regular. The moon seemed to recede and sharpen in focus.

John decided he was feeling good—absolutely bone tired and unstrung—loose, but good. Everything was numb but his hand.

– OSCAR –

(2005)

———

OSCAR

(2005)

Oscar. Yeah. I got one. Kinda. Sorta. You could more accurately say I am in possession of an Oscar statuette. He looks like all the others, a little over a foot high. Surprisingly heavy, close to nine pounds. He's a little battered. He got broken at the ankles once when I was still stupid enough to bring him out at parties, but my friend Rudy at Rudy's Machine Shop fixed him just fine. You can hardly see the hairline crack. Also, he comes equipped with a curse.

Not exactly my Oscar because my name's not on the plaque, though it should be. What it says is:

Best Live Action Short Film

"Laps"

Todd Griffith & Mary O'Hearn
Producers

Todd was in film school with me and loved a short story of mine, "Individual Medley." It's about a failed swimmer, an Olympic contender who burns out but later starts swimming again to cope with a painful divorce. Todd saw something there—childhood success, then failure, and Americans' love of exercise as therapy—that he thought would make a short movie. He had a lot of money, and so did his wife, Mary. I said sure.

They weren't the usual East Coast rich kids, the kind Californians love to send back to Connecticut after six years with a depleted trust fund, newfound humility—or at least a sense of bafflement—and a heroin habit. Todd wasn't a great writer, but he had an eye for talent, he worked hard, and Mary did have talent as a film editor. The handshake deal we had was that for the story rights, I'd get a co-producer credit: Todd Griffith / Mary O'Hearn / Dale Davis.

Todd spent his last year writing the script. I rewrote it in two weeks and was on to other projects. They took two years to shoot the movie, and Todd was smart. He got retired guys—the best in the biz, including some of our teachers—to help him. He got Esther Williams's cameraman to shoot the water sequences. The money showed. I was in Nicaragua when they found out they were nominated. That was when I found out I was no longer a producer. Mary found out the same time I did, and she was as pissed off as I was.

When they won, Todd went completely off the rails. He slept with the goddamn statuette. He and Mary separated within six months, and Mary considered actually treating Oscar as a child when it came to the divorce, seeking custody just to bring Todd to his senses, but Todd was beyond that. He was on to his dream project—a science fiction/noir mashup that none of a succession of agents could reduce to a pitchable combo. The best one managed was, "It's kind of like *The Two Jakes* go to *Dune*."

The worst part was that now that Todd was an Oscar winner, he no longer felt that he should have to invest any of his own money in his projects, beyond the money he spent hosting nightly parties at his new apartment at the Chateau Beachwood, a mock Normandy castle built by Warner Bros. to house starlets in the '40s in Beachwood Canyon. Corner of Beachwood

Drive and Scenic Avenue. Marilyn Monroe, Garbo, and Diet-
rich once lived there. And so did a fictional character, China
Blue, an amateur hooker played by Kathleen Turner in one of
Ken Russell's worst movies, *Crimes of Passion*. Todd loved that
movie and China Blue's apartment, where Anthony Perkins
is killed with a sharpened metal vibrator named Superman. It
was the apartment he insisted on. Todd had what he was now
calling his "golden panty-dropper" installed in a glass case atop
the fireplace, and soon the Holly-Polloi—the freaks, the weekly
famous, those with hair nature never imagined, the tattooed
mouth-breathers, the sister-acts—descended.

Beachwood Canyon was used to a fairly high level of dissipa-
tion; it is the road to the Hollywood sign. Nathanael West called
the place "Pinyon Canyon" in *The Day of the Locust* and located
Homer Simpson and Faye Greener there. Aldous Huxley hosted
psychedelic parties in the mid-fifties in upper Beachwood. Todd
managed, in two months, to piss off every neighbor in the building, including some notorious degenerates, and was on a first-
name basis with the local paramedics, both day and night shift.

The bills were so bad that his family finally staged an inter-
vention. Todd only agreed on the Malibu Rehab if Oscar came
along, and it was definitely a point of contention with the staff
there. Some of them wanted to let him keep the cocaine and take
away the statue. When he made the jump, Oscar went with him:
eighty feet down. Oscar survived, as bronze will. Todd did not.
Those beautiful cliffs and the view they provided had been a big
selling point for Malibu Rehab.

Mary collected Oscar, but by this time she felt he was cursed.
At first, she left him out on display at her apartment, but he
weirded out her boyfriend and friends in different ways. And
someone was always trying to walk off with him. It seemed to
be a compulsion. When she put him away, they thought that
was weird too. Her career wasn't going well. She made some

bad choices, turning down an indie film for a shot at her first studio picture. The studio picture blew up when the two stars started fighting and one backed out and the indie turned out to be *Drugstore Cowboy*, which made it a compound mistake. She would have worked for years with that credit. Then her boyfriend dumped her and added insult by moving in with a film student in her twenties, and Mary decided that the curse of Oscar had taken its toll. When she passed him on to me, on her way to the Ashram where she still resides, she said, "You don't want to own him. So, let's make this a loan." She wrote it down. Bless her.

I've been grateful for that over the years, when two ex-wives sued for possession, but mostly, because I also believe the guy is cursed. If he wasn't still Mary's, things might be worse.

When I first got Oscar, I flaunted him. My name wasn't on the plaque, and that required some explanation, but the film was based on my story, which gave me some bragging rights, and the widow, I explained, had done the honorable thing.

I learned pretty quickly not to leave him out at parties or un-attended. There was just something irresistible about even a mi-nor-league Oscar that made hardcore cinema fanatics—foamers, we call them—want to take him home or severely damage him. He had his ankles broken by a very drunken Polish cinematogra-pher who concluded a long rant on the evils of capitalism and the corruption of the academy—*Driving Miss Daisy* had just beaten the un-nominated *Do the Right Thing* for Best Picture—by pounding the poor boy's base against the mantel while weeping. I was a bit conflicted that night since I agreed with him.

After that, Oscar only came out for small gatherings. For casual dinner parties, football games, and meetings with people I could trust, he resided in the refrigerator, to surprise people when they went for more wine or a beer.

For more formal dinner parties or actual dates, Oscar stood dis-creetly in the bathroom behind the liquid soap dispenser. Invariably, after a flush, there was a five-minute pause for posing before the mirror and afterward, for first-timers, the question: "Is that real?"

He did change my life. The cause of two of my marriages or, more accurately, two of my divorces, he raised expectations that were never going to be fulfilled.

After the '88 strike and what went down with the showrunner, in the years that followed as I watched the long, slow swirl of my career circle the porcelain flume, I began, like Mary, to believe in the curse. But I couldn't get rid of him. He still meant something, a tangible memory of who I'd almost been. And he still separated me from the crowd.

Over the years I would test this, particularly when I was broke and at a low ebb. Oscar and I would go out and hit a few bars together. The results were always entertaining.

Eventually, I developed some protocols.

Number one: the chain. If you don't have the chain, someone, somewhere will try to steal Oscar. That's just what happens. They think he's valuable. They don't know you can't sell him. Not legally. The Academy's buyback is a buck. And he's not gold. Just gold wash. The actual metal value all depends on the price of gold. Right now, fifty-five bucks. The chain, light steel, small padlock saves a lot of hassle. Before I thought of it, I once had to cold-cock someone with Oscar. That was a moment.

Number two: bar selection. Nothing too high-end. Oscar does not go to Beverly Hills. Oscar does not visit Musso-Franks. Nor does Oscar go to total dive bars. Oscar likes to go to bars where the clientele may include knowledgeable movie buffs, but not too knowledgeable. Mainly, career drinkers.

Here's how it typically goes:

(Interior—night)

A tired but handsome man sits down at

a bar. He reaches into a satchel beside
him and retrieves an Oscar statuette,
which is chained to his wrist, sets it
carefully on the bar.

DALE

I'm broke, but tomorrow I'm going
to sell my Oscar to a collector for
$12,500. Isn't that a hell of a note.

GUY DOWN THE BAR

I thought you couldn't sell those
things.

DALE

Legally, no. But as I said, I'm broke.

40ISH BLONDE (ATTRACTIVE)

Can I touch him?

DALE

Sure.

BARTENDER

(noting the interest that Dale and Oscar are drawing) Let me buy you the

first one, Pal. What are you drinking?

DALE

Double Basil Hayden, rocks, splash of
water. (Bartender winces)

40ISH BLONDE

Are you Todd Griffith?

DALE

That's me.

40ISH BLONDE

Where's Mary?

DALE

She died.

40ISH BLONDE

Oh, that's sad. Can I get a photo with
you and Oscar?

GUY DOWN THE BAR

What was it like, the night you won?

And it will go on like that, making new friends, some I might even bring home, but probably not tonight. Oscar stays chained. I will enjoy a lot of free drinks.

We'll come home. Light a fire. Few more drinks. Enough to forget the rest of the day or encase it in the kind of melancholy glow that lets you watch it the way you would a sunset. Oscar on the hearth, gleaming. At some point I'll give him his traditional toast. "They tell me you're cast from bronze and covered with gold, but I know better. You're the stuff that dreams are made of." Then I'll put him back in the closet. He's too tough to face in the morning.

- NOT OLIVER STONE -

(2006)

NOT OLIVER STONE

(2006)

I WAS SITTING BY THE BACK BAR IN THE SHOWROOM at the House of Blues. This is the Sunset Strip House of Blues, and if you know the joint, you know what a feat it was to be sitting, because there are only a few quasi-chairs. There is a herd of stools with no backs, but that's not sitting. Basically, at the House of Blues, they like you to be standing, which is another way of saying they like you to be young.

There are six quasi-chairs in the back of the showroom, six tall stools with backs. HoB chairs. They back up against a narrow table that the idlers behind us use as a rail to lean against.

We old guys congregate there, clutching our drinks because that table is really too narrow to set a drink on, and if you did, it would be behind you so you couldn't always see it, and unattended drinks, even brown ones like mine, tend to vanish within this young and agile crowd.

When a chair opens up, there's usually a lot of fast-fiftyish shuffling, which tonight is appropriate because tonight is reggae night. Everton Blender was on stage, keeping up that slow churning beat so that when a chair opened up, and the old guys bobbed and lunged toward it, it looked like they were appropriately dancing. Everton Blender is very Black and not very tall and not very good, but he has a kind of staff, a tall stick like an upside-down

L that has horny spikes, or spikey horns, on the L part. And the stick, which he uses to direct and clear space with, is impressive, and so is his band and the two jellyworm chick singers who are not only not intimidated by the staff but don't pay attention at all to Everton Blender.

Toots and the Maytals were up next, and that was who most of us were waiting for, but because the band and the undulant backups were so good, we put up with Everton Blender. Mostly you can't understand a word he says or sings except for Jah and Jamaica and Good Spirit and Selassie, which are repeated with every song, either in the song or in the introduction, with thrusts of the stick.

Rastafarians aren't any sillier than Mormons, theologically, but their music is better. I won't listen to ten seconds of the Mormon Tabernacle Choir, and I'll sit through an evening of Everton Blender because of that beat. Also, their dope is better and the contact high floating back from this choogling crowd almost makes sense of it all. I know Everton thinks or hopes that we come to listen because of Jah, but we don't. It's like a cult of really good barbers who also just happen to believe that the earth is flat and assume you're there to hear about the flatness of the earth and incidentally get a haircut.

In the middle of all this there was an odd lull. A bodybuilder-looking guy in front of us with porcupine dreadlocks had lit an enormous spliff and waved it like incense for all of us.

Nobody paid him any attention, this after a waitress called security's attention to a frontward-baseball-cap guy who lit up a Lucky Strike and held it cupped, waving it in his hand between sneaked puffs. They threw him out, and then the lull set in, and the chair to the right of me opened up, and the chair to the left of me opened up, and no one rushed to fill them. Into the middle of all this walked a guy, real old guy, maybe fifty-eight, who looked familiar, kind of a potato-shaped head and pale peeled-potato face, jowly with a veiny potato nose. Everything else about him was black—atonal black coiled hair, black stubble, black eyes, black pants, black shirt, and an Italian black leather jacket that looked like scalloped armor. The jacket creaked expensively as he walked and even more as he sat to my left, boosting up and bumping down on the tall chair. I ignored him until I realized he was inclining himself in my direction. Slowly I turned to face him. It was a really familiar face, now about three inches from my own. He didn't hold out his hand or anything, but he was clearly introducing himself.

"Hey," he said. "I'm Not Oliver Stone." There was a pause as he reeled his face back. "I just want to make that clear."

"What?" I said, a little reflexively.

"Because of what's going to happen," Not Oliver Stone said. "Because of what always happens. Sooner or later, someone is going to ask you to confirm or deny, and now that I've told you, you can say, 'No, he's Not Oliver Stone.'"

"I wouldn't want to talk to anyone like that," I told him, again a little reflexively.

"Well, you might have to because it always happens," he said. He straightened up and went stone-faced on me, blank as a bulb.

And it pretty much did happen the way he said it would. Inside a minute he was surrounded by three teenage blondes who all had the same two-dimensional face, except for the smartest, skinniest one who had a nose and might have been more like thirty. She'd dragged a stool with her and wedged it next to Not Oliver Stone. The other two danced around, flitted off for conferences, and returned. I couldn't make out the conversation, but Not Oliver was enjoying himself, almost reclining. Eventually there was a pause, and she repeated herself, and I could hear her say, "So what do you do?"

Not Oliver Stone looked at her significantly and then, significantly, he turned away. He turned to me. "So," he says to me, "what do you do?"

I was pretty sure by now that he might be Oliver Stone, but this being LA and most particularly the Sunset Strip, I couldn't really be sure. He could be pretending to be pretending that he was who he said he wasn't.

Well, fuck it. I saw that this might be my only chance to get my drink refilled. "I do government work," I said.

Not Oliver Stone nodded sagely. "You work for the government," he said. His eyebrows rippled and strained like woolly bear caterpillars stuck on flypaper. "Ahh, in what aspect would that be? Of government."

"I do government work"—I was running with Jesus now—"but I can't talk about it."

Not Oliver Stone nodded sagely again but then ruined the whole wisdom-effect thing he had going with a ludicrous wink and simper that turned into a nod toward the stage and Everton Blender. "Immigration maybe?" His voice was an augmented whisper, some sort of special effect. "Would that be the kind of work you do?"

"Immigration?" I said. "That's kind of insulting. Makes me think that maybe you haven't been cleared. All I can tell you is that I'm on the scientific end of things."

He was clearly interested now. He air-elbowed the skinny blonde who was trying to insinuate herself and then hissed away a waitress who was trying to present him with a green drink on a silver plate. "What appellation?" he asked, "NIH? NESC? SCI?" The waitress tried to present again. She bobbed upward—clearly she'd worked there a long time; she had those rubbed features, always catching herself on a slurred vowel and recovering, "Man'... man'ger's compliments. Your gimlet." She placed the tray under his nose. A mistake. He sniffed and tipped it over. "I said Ruuskvi Standarte. Pre-Wall. Kremlin reserve. This was negotiated. If you don't have it, just tell me. I would adjust. But I hate these kinds of surprises. Does Mikhi no longer work here?"

I held out my empty glass. "JD rocks, splash water," but she was moccasinning away, stemmed glass rolling on the silver tray. Not Oliver refocused on me with real heat. "You're not ND-NAL, are you?"

"As far as I know," I said, "that organization does not exist. If tortured, I would still deny its existence."

That was what he wanted to hear. "Tell me your name."

D. Dale Davis is what it is. I added the D. a few years ago when that all made sense. Like the tattoo. But that's not what I tell him. I don't want him to recall the name later or the scripts of mine he's spurned.

"E. Eddie Edwards," was what I told him.

"E. Eddie," Not Oliver Stone said, "you don't have to confirm or deny, but just tell me where you are in the process. Have you started sampling yet? Are lists being made?"

Why not. "Officially," I said, "the Administration is against human cloning. They have issued that policy statement."

Not Oliver gleefully waited for me to finish. He was nearly bouncing. "I knew it. I knew it."

The listless waitress appeared again, but she was up now. She stood well away, proffering her tray and its luminous green drink. "Ruuskvi Standarte," she said, "Mikhi guarantees on the life of his dogs." Her diction was auditionally crisp.

Not Oliver ignored her. He was over-focused on me. He looked like a bloodhound on point. "Around 1986," I said, "Defense got a little jealous of Interior. A gas-testing site near Camp Pendleton got shut down because of Spifex Catalina, a rare and useless moth. Interior actually curtailed important military operations by claiming a need to protect endangered species or natural resources. We lost a bomb run in Nevada to rhyolite miners. That was humiliating. Some of us in Defense recognized that we had no natural resources, which was the Holy Mother Grail, politically speaking."

The waitress had listened intently, focusing as closely as Not Oliver. When I paused, she downed the gimlet. "Can I get you guys anything else?" she said. Not Oliver blinked. I raised a finger. "JD rocks double," but she'd already gone abstract, far beyond waitress. She went transcendental wobbly and then gathered. "That's not Ruuskvi Standarte," she said and tottered off.

"When cloning became feasible," I continued, "that seemed to us to be an area of opportunity. A way into the natural resources pool. We wanted our own area of sympathetic response. It seemed to us that we had that in the gene pool of Great Americans, dead and living. How could you not want Albert Einstein on your side in the event of another external threat, rogue state, or emerging power?"

"The Post-Dolly syndrome." Not Oliver was smug now. Clearly he had researchers, about the random level one finds in the movie business. I continued. "What sold Congress were the possibilities, once we explained that beyond initial cloning, a breeding program could be established. You could bring Einstein back as Albert, or with a twist of the test tube, so to speak, as Alberta. The sizzle we sold them was: Suppose you could approach the next imminent conflict with the offspring of Alberta Einstein and Edmund Teller. Scientific genius without premature humanistic tendencies. Drive, ambition, an appreciation of Realpolitik without waffling.

"We are written into the budget as a single submarine, the USS *Bear Bryant*. One point eight billion dollars that will never reach New Groton, Connecticut."

"That would be one ugly baby," Not Oliver said.

"In more ways than one," I replied. The waitress was back, completely furious now and focused, with a full tray of gimlets, which she hurled at Not Oliver from ten feet. "You bastard," she screamed. "You don't even remember me. Melissa! Melissa!" As the glasses chimed and crashed around us, security swept in. Onstage, Everton Blender took note of the parting of the crowd and raised his stick and shook it toward us. "All for Jah. All for Selassie." The biggest security guy waved a hand to Everton Blender as they dragged the waitress away and set down four new gimlets at Not Oliver's elbow. Back at her station, security released her to her peers, and they gathered and held her. "Hang in, Tori," the bartender said. The other waitresses patted and crooned.

What I said was, "Once the budget was in place and the library was established, we swept through the scientific community. Basically, anyone with a PhD is in the bank. Then, since the money was in place and we wanted to justify the new submarine, we started to look at the arts."

"Because somebody," Not Oliver resonated (that augmented speech box thing was on again), "needs to entertain those scientists!"

"That's when we ran into problems," I said. "Because it turns out that while no congressman would dare opine about science or scientists, even the meekest has an opinion about art and artists. They started drawing up lists."

"Everybody's a critic," Not Oliver Stone said, not unsadly.

"Oh, don't worry," I said. "You made some of the lists. The problem was, there were so many lists, they ended up with an A-list, B-list, C-list, and an In-Case-of-National-Emergency-list."

"Am I A-list?" The caterpillars were crawling again.

I was enjoying it now. "Kinda B-plus," I said. "You did really well in Wisconsin."

His brow unfurrowed. Total Frida Kahlo look. "I am on the DNA B-list?" Too late I understood what the unfurrowed brow meant—he'd gone into studio survivor mode. Concentration, for him, clearly meant absence of thought, just reaction. It was a gift, the kind that gets movies made.

What I expected was that he would ask how much it would cost to move up to A-list. And then after more lack of thought, how much it would cost to demote a few friends and mentors to B. That wasn't happening. He went from reactive to smug in a heartbeat. "Thank you for your, uhhhh, expertise." There was a slight pause as he tried to remember my name, gave up, and went back to total Stone-face. I was looking at Mount Rushmore. "But the technical advisers from *Platoon* are now flag-rank and higher. I think I can sort this out."

I lost it. Couldn't help it. So unfair. He would be moving up the list, if there was one, by morning. If there wasn't a list, one would be created, and he could take credit, and I would be just another Idea Man he'd ripped off before I'd even known that I had an idea.

"*Platoon* sucked," I whispered. "A medieval miracle play. They could have been wearing signs—Good, Evil. So did *JFK* and *Wall Street*. *The Doors* was an abomination!" I was yelling now. The crowd had cratered around us and was leaning in; Not Oliver was clearly enjoying the attention. Even Everton Blender paused. "The only good movie you ever made," I shouted, "was *Salvador*, and that was only because James Woods took it over and wrote his own dialogue and directed himself!"

The imploded crowd whispered and sizzled, but Not Oliver didn't react except that his eyebrows seemed to have disappeared. I was facing a brow as broad and placid as Orson Welles's dying Kane. I hated that unseemly metaphor. If there was anyone who was a non-icon, it was this guy.

What he said was, "Yes."

"Yes," he said. "People tell me that a lot...and it may even be true, but of course..." I knew what he was going to say. I despaired. "But of course," he continued, "I'm Not Oliver Stone."

He crooked a finger, and security moved in. As they closed on me, I could see Everton Blender waving his stick in benediction. "Ahhhhhh, the Righteous Mon," Everton sang.

"You fucked up every major theme of my generation," I wailed. They pinned my arms and started to duckwalk me away. Not Oliver held up a hand. "Turn him," he said. "Stand him up." They held me and stood me up.

"Yesssss," Not Oliver said, "your brilliant Mr. Woodssss. He went on to quite a career. *Diggstown*. Ever see that one, hmmmmm? I'm sure the payment for that performance allowed him to do some *worthy* play or independent feature." Worthy was a curse on his lips. I reeled backward. Not Oliver dismissed me with a flick of his hand and turned his attention to the stage.

"I got to get me one of those sticks," he said to the skinny blonde. "Be great on the set."

They rolled me out like a hand truck, my heels bumping on the steps. As we passed the corner of the back bar, a bristly bartender, big, wrestler-looking guy wearing a T-shirt covered with Cyrillic script, came over and nodded at me encouragingly. I was close enough now to read his nametag, MIKHI, and the English translation of his shirt: Georgia on My Mind. Mikhi winked at me and brought a magnum-sized bottle out from beneath the bar. More Cyrillic script.

"Ruuskvi Standarte," Mikhi said, "the real thing, and he never get a drop of it. I make sure."

"Tell him James Woods is on the A-list," I said.

Mikhi raised a fist for me, and his face clenched with some emotion I didn't recognize. Enthusiasm? Solidarity? He shook the fist for me. "We do what we can, kidski."

- QUALITY OF LIFE -

(2007)

QUALITY OF LIFE

(2007)

THREE O'CLOCK OF THE AFTERNOON AT MY USUAL haunt, Carleton Liquors, and I bump up against Chief Bratton's *Quality of Life*. The chief's high concept, evolved and refined in his previous tour of duty, New York City, boils down to: *Sweat the Small Stuff.*

CB believes that if you fix the broken windows, arrest public urinators and defecators, untolerate graffiti, i.e., improve the quality of neighborhood life, the big-time crime—rapes, robberies, assaults, murders—will also dwindle.

The way that *I* find out about the new policies is with the shift change at the Hollywood Cop Shop. In the past, a shift change meant at least an hour of uninterrupted peace; I planned my day accordingly. The Day Shift comes in from wherever they have been hiding, and the Night Shift needs at least an hour to find their hidey holes. Cop morale in Hollywood has been so bad for so long that we Degenerates have come to depend on it. It started with a batch of bad busts and wrongful death cases. A decade of multi-million-dollar judgments made Hollywood Division gun-shy. Arrests meant trouble, or at least paperwork, and a generation of cops decided to hang out and hide out until the pension was in view.

But today, shift changes, *Bang, Zoom.* Black and white pulls up and blocks the driveway, and two energetic Latina cops get out, braced to let Herman and me know that we represent blight on the quality of life on our particular corner of Gower and Carleton Way. Herman is nodding in his wheelchair in the corner of the lot, and I am sitting quietly in my Saturn reading the sports page, a discreet tallboy of Rainier Ale nestled in the open console, pretty well hidden, I thought, by the paper. In the side mirror, I can see Officer Hernandez—her name plaque glows like neon—take a stance, holding up her walkie-talkie like a weightlifter and reading my license number forcefully into the microphone. Her partner—gotta be six feet tall, que nutrition will do in a generation—Officer Lopez is at the passenger side open window. "GOOD AFTERNOON, SIR!" Officer Lopez booms. "MAY I ASK IF THAT IS AN ALCOHOLIC BEVERAGE YOU HAVE THERE IN YOUR CENTER CONSOLE?"

I roll the newspaper and hold up the guilty can.

"AND AM I CORRECT IN SURMISING THAT THIS IS AN OPEN CONTAINER, ONE YOU HAVE BEEN DRINKING FROM?"

I nod.

"THEN MAY I ASK YOU TO PLEASE STEP OUT OF THE VEHICLE, SIR!"

Herman chooses the wrong time to come to life. Herman is small, Black, and bald, surprisingly clean-shaven—I heard once that a sister visited and maintained him. Usually he is collapsed on himself, but in my defense, his head pops up. He drops his empty Night Train bottle with a loud clink and rolling clatter and wheels out. "You don't gotta get out of the car, unless they got a warrant, 'cause you're not driving. This *ain't* the street. This *ain't* they jurisdiction. I been through this one. I know the law on this one."

I look at the posted sign on the wall in front of my windshield, with its numerical citation of the City Code, "Drinking of Alcoholic Beverages is prohibited," and know no good can come of this.

Officers Hernandez and Lopez stand up from the holster-gun-clasped-crouches that Herman's dropped bottle provoked, turn, and stare at my advocate.

"This here is private property," Herman says, fierce and assured as a Neo-Con. No good can come from this. Herman may even be right. He is bright, and when he was ambulatory, he did enough jail time to really study law. I wouldn't know. I just want this to go away. The open container ticket is sixty-five bucks. I've paid it before. It's an occupational expense.

I am known as a good citizen. I do pay my taxes. Every day, when I park at Carleton Liquors, the first hungry, smokeless, drinkless soul to reach my fender knows that I am good for a buck. I'm glad to pay my tax and sip and read in peace. Chief Bratton has disturbed this peace.

Herman rolls up to my window, flanked by the swiveling cops. "Don't get out the car," Herman hisses.

Easy for Herman to say. Herman is mostly invulnerable, as close to a Superhero as you will find on the corner of Gower and Carleton Way. He is drunk and disabled, smells like a hot, closed-up bungalow with a week-dead widow and eighty cats, and, as the entire Hollywood Division knows, is capable of on-demand urination, defecation, or vomitation, that is, if anyone would be stupid enough to arrest him and seat him in the back of a police cruiser—which the arresting officers are obligated to clean. His personal odor will cling to the seats of a squad car, like the smell of curry in the stairwells of immigrant apartments, for years. If you touch him, the essential essence of Herman guarantees that even after a week of showers, baths, and saunas, nostrils will flare when you enter a room. Plus, there is the fucking wheelchair to deal with. Herman is invulnerable.

"Trust me on this, Davis," Herman whispers. "I know the law on this one."

"The LAW! The LAW!" An unmistakable screeching voice penetrates our lawyer-client conference. Mona, preceded by her familiar taint, patchouli and sulfur, struts onto our stage, today wearing a red vinyl halter, black *Raider* sweatpants, and a lime tutu. At her best, trolling for clients drunk enough to focus on her low-rent implants and ignore her prominent Adam's apple and bristling jaw, Mona looks like a Sunday Crow. She has a bright and cognizant eye and a need for shining objects. I should probably mention here that Mona and I have a history. She is no respecter of honest taxpayers. Whenever Mona reels into view, she wants money. *Gimme ten dollar* is her opening offer. *Gimme a dollar, bitch!* is her counteroffer. *I will FUCK you up!* is her default mode.

Today, however, she is trying out a hideous parody of an honest and outraged citizen, nearly davening before Officers Lopez and Hernandez, her hands fluttering about her head. "I am so glad the law has finally arrived, some justice has come to Dodge City. I have called in, again and again, from my house here on Carleton Way—that's 1831 Carleton Way." A collapsed shingled two-story that went down in the earthquake of '92, with squabbling heirs who can't decide what to do with the property. Mona has a tent pitched there. "And as a taxpayer"—Mona may sometimes pay state sales tax on what she hasn't shoplifted—"I have been outraged by the public drinking of intoxicants that goes on here in this parking lot. I am so glad you officers have finally answered my calls."

Officers Lopez and Hernandez stare at Mona, whose fluttering hand speed has just gone from jitter to blur. Herman meantime has backed away from my door to better view Mona's soliloquy. He raises a finger, cocks his thumb. and points it at her. "I fucking object," Herman yells. "She irrelevant."

Mona wheels on him. "And you, you nasty little Tiny Tim, don't know shit about the law. If you did, you'd know this drunk in the car here about to go to jail." Mona's eyes look like pin-wheels on springs. I can't even imagine what she is on; she does have one customer who pays with his dead mother's weird and outdated prescriptions.

Herman counters, "It's you who don't know shit, you lank-stick. Worse this is a ticket. Open container. And if he lissen to me and stay in the car, he won't even get that."

Mona nearly levitates in triumph. "Roll that crinkly dwarf out of here! You too low to see it, crippboy, but your fool here has his keys in the ignition. That be drinking AND driving." She smiles evilly at me. "A 5-0-2 to you, Davis!" It's true the keys are in the ignition, and a rising sense of dread gathers at the base of my spine.

"The car not running," Herman says.

Mona cocks a hand behind her ear, "What I hear?" In the silence, the low murmur of Jim Rome arises from my speakers.

"He got the radio on," Herman says. "So what?"

"That mean the key engage. It not off. That's the law!"

Herman actually looks upset, like Mona may know some-thing. Officers Hernandez and Lopez, who have followed this arcane legal exchange in silence, seem to be deciding what to do next. Then Mona helps them decide.

Mona flutters her eyelashes at them, clasps her hands to her bosom, preening, and says, "I believe Mona is right. I believe that is the law. Please tell me, Officers. Dears. Is that the law?"

Officer Lopez raises a palm, asking for silence. Mona quiets but continues to bat eyelashes, and Officer Lopez, looking directly into Mona's spinning eyes, says, "May I see some identification, sir?"

Mona sucks in a breath, and her eyes stop spinning, momen-tarily. "What did you say?"

"I'll need to see some identification, sir."

Mona cocks a hip and throws out her modest bosom. It's the only tasteful thing about Mona, really. She didn't go for the obvious gazongas. They are proportional. They may even be hormonal rather than implants. She throws out her modest bosom and says, "You must apologize," and then her red eyes start their slow roll, then a spiral, and Mona screams, "Apologize, bitch! Or I will *fuck* you up!" and drops into a would-be karate chop fighting stance.

Officers Lopez and Hernandez don't waste any motion. Hernandez drops Mona with one meaty arm, Lopez rolls her on the pavement and pull-ties the plastic cuffs, while Hernandez begins the litany, "You have the right to remain silent, you have the right to an attorney..." Not even reading from the little card that most cops bring out for the occasion, from memory, the new breed of professional, and in a half a minute, Mona, trussed, kicking, and screaming, is stashed flat in the back of the cruiser, and Officer Hernandez has taken the wheel. Officer Lopez reaches a long arm through the passenger-side window, plucks my Rainier Tallboy from the center console with a thumb and forefinger, and then pours it out on the pavement while addressing me. "I hope," Officer Lopez says, "you will have the good sense to be gone from here by the time we resume our shift."

I nod solemnly. "Yes, Officer."

"And in the future, you need to do your drinking at home, because this will be our first stop every shift." She crumples the can with one squeeze and tosses it in one of the cardboard boxes the Carleton Liquors proprietors set out for empties. A new day in Dodge. Her Sam Brown belt and holster creak leatherally as she adjusts them on her hip and then strides away. As soon as Officer Lopez has her seatbelt cinched, Hernandez cranks the key. I think both Herman and I are impressed at the way we are now ignored.

Officer Hernandez brodies the steering wheel, looking over her shoulder in a perfect veteran move, and the Cruiser backs out in a half-circle and shoots off down Carleton Way. We can see

Mona's heels kicking, through the back window. The lime green tutu is now around her ankles.

Herman and I look at each other, and I get out of the Saturn, go into Carleton Liquors, and return with a fresh Rainier for me and a Night Train for Herman. I crack the cap and hand the cold, sweating bottle over to Herman. "Your retainer, sir."

He lifts it, sips it squinting, and a little of the orange wine spills and pools on his lap. "Justice be served," Herman says.

– "WRITTEN OUT" –

A STORY BY DALE DAVIS

(2007)

— "WRITTEN OUT" —

A STORY BY DALE DAVIS

(2007)

"WRITTEN OUT"

A STORY BY DALE DAVIS

(2007)

DAHO SLIM ROLLED HIS TOOTHPICK AROUND THE
whole course of his mouth. He flipped the pick a full turn in
the air and caught it on his furled tongue, a practiced move that
would have impressed if there had been anyone there to witness.

It was high noon in Killarney, Texas, and even the snakes
had gone limp. Down Main Street from the depot, in the foot of
shade cast by the courthouse steps, the Mayor's berserker terrier
lay inches away from his nighttime mortal enemy, the School-
teacher's marmalade cat. The cat's tail flicked and tapped the terrier on the nose. The dog only whimpered in his dream, and a
back leg twitched. That's how goddamn hot it was.

The town had been named by its first resident, an Irishman
who was reminded of his home county. How this was possible
was hard to figure. There was no greenery in Killarney. Green
could be painted, but it blistered and peeled in a month. Cactus aside, there was no other green. Later residents surmised that
Seamus Clary had enjoyed hallucinations. He'd awakened in the
place after his fellow teamsters threw him off the freight wagon
for hygienic reasons. Seamus might have landed on his head be-

cause he awakened with a sense of purpose foreign to his nature.

He staked the land, registered it, and then drank himself to death in a three-month binge of celebratory triumph. Later residents, displaying either a lack of ambition or rudimentary real estate sales sense, hadn't bothered to change the name. Unpainted, unkempt, the roofs still unshingled, Killarney survived by virtue of its location along the railroad right-of-way and position of county seat.

Idaho Slim, like most involuntary visitors, was not impressed.

The only fresh thing about the place was a stack of new railroad ties, reeking of creosote under the baking sun. The peeling gray planks of the freight platform Slim leaned against gapped and twisted against rusted lifted nails. Flaking red paint and white trim drifted down like dandruff around Slim. A dozen tumbleweeds, stalled when the morning wind died, hunkered in the dust waiting for the sun to stop hammering them on this anvil.

Carefully lifting his toothpick out of harm's way, Slim spat. The phlegm shrank in the air, like a bead of water dancing on a hot skillet, and never reached the ground.

"I am not impressed," Slim called out. Not even a parched echo responded. The Mayor's recumbent terrier whimpered in his heat dream and twitched closer to the coolth of the marmalade cat.

Three hours later, and Slim was still not impressed. The first inch of eastbound shade was struggling toward the street, just the gable's shadow. "Goddamn," Slim said, "Something needs to happen. Something better happen. Something had better happen. Soon. Goddamn."

He spat again, and this time it reached the ground, where it sizzled and crisped. By four thirty Slim was expectorating into a damp spot. The roof's shadow had reached the middle of Main, and the false-fronted sheds along the street seemed to sag and yawn with relief.

At the end of the street, a distant figure stirred into view. Slim squinted but couldn't bring the figure into distinction. A small kick of dust surrounded it. As the figure moved into perspective, Slim focused on a dragging panted leg. Gabardine. The leg flailed wide, dug in, and the dust swirled up. Slim shoved down on the right-hand Colt until the holster creaked. The nearer the Gabardine man came, the higher the dust rose. Slim gripped the pistol, prepared to hoist.

The man stopped about twenty feet away, and the brown cloud obscured him. From the hovering dust a voice emerged, high and unnatural, like a jockey's, or a girl gymnast's, and the rhythm was a litany of complaint. "What the hell? It's only four thirty. Is there something you know that I don't? Who was it told you different? I'm not blaming you, now. Are we on golden time?"

The dust descended, and Slim faced his inquisitor, who looked happy. His face was as open and innocent as a pansy. He must've been an orphan, Slim thought. The man lifted his hat and then, with two hands, his right leg. He shook it. "Heighdy," he said. "I'm Timmy, the Town Gimp."

He waggled his leg again. "It's an honorary position. I'm not really crippled." Slim didn't respond. It was a career move. As part of his campaign to move up from Sidekick, he'd attempted a new moniker, "Silent Slim," and he was practicing it now. He would talk to the Mayor, if he had to. Maybe the Marshall. But he'd be damned if he would respond to any lower echelon stereotype. Timmy was sizing him up. Slim could feel his stare. He hoisted the Colt from his left holster to eye level and sighted on the Bank weathervane, a brass vulture with a coin in its beak.

"Well. Excuse me. Excuse me all to hell," Timmy piped. "I didn't realize you was The Stranger. No, sir. My lapse. I'll give you the traditional welcome now you have revealed yourself." Timmy dragged his leg in the dirt and gaped. "Why, you must be a *Staranger* in town."

The *problem*, Slim thought, was that in order to promote his new name *he* needed a Sidekick. It made no sense to *say*, "I'm Silent Slim." He could imagine what that line would lead to. It would be a real crowd-pleaser, a real exploding stove. The questioner, probably a Gimp like this one, or the Town Drunk, would get to keep saying, "I can't hear you. What was the name?" and he'd finally have to shout, "Silent Slim!"

They'd love it. Footprints on the ceiling, all the people all of the time, but where would that leave Slim? If he had his own Sidekick, or even just a Daily, the guy could announce him. Point with awe maybe. A Daily might even be better, some passing stranger who, because of Slim's renown, could say to the importunate questioner, "Don't you *know* who that is? Why, that's *Silent Slim!*" Slim could almost feel the hiss and shiver of the italics, the stamp of the exclamation. If it was one of the really good Old-Time Daily Players, they might even let him throw in a stutter. Then the Gimp or the Drunk would get to do a Take.

Whur's 'at goddamn train? Slim thought. He wished he could have said it. It sounded good to him. He knew a good line even if they didn't give him many lines. The Gimp was still gaping at him, so Slim turned round. It was hard being tall and smart and looking better than you should for the part. They had to shoot around you a lot. He'd spent a lot of time in ditches looking eye to eye with heroes standing on boxes. Time was running out, Slim thought.

Which made Slim think to look at the Town Clock. This clock, an approximation of a frontier fort watchtower necessarily made of cactus rather than logs, had faces on four sides but on three sides the hands were painted on. The hands on the face that looked down on Main Street did move, but whimsically. At the end of each hand—they should have been called arms—badly rendered shamrocks pointed the time. They looked like green boxing gloves. They were moving now, as Slim watched, shifting jerkily from 5:17 to five minutes before six. It looked as though someone inside the cabin was moving the hands separately.

The Gimp popped open his pocket watch and compared it to the clock. "Almost time. I guess you bein' a stranger, you didn't know we start at five."

"That says six," Slim was about to say, but then he remembered, and wordlessly held up one hand and one finger. The Gimp held up the watch and faced it so Slim could see. It read 4:57.

"That clock is wrong," the Gimp said. "So wrong. I can't even begin to tell you. Goddamn Grips."

Down the street the swing doors of the Saloon exploded outward, and a cannonball of rags sailed out, bounced, and rolled to a stop near their feet. The ball unwound and stood, swaying.

Slim looked down at the tattered man; his faded bottle-green suit and lemon brocade vest were alive with sprouting threads. Miraculously, the man popped a collapsible brushed beaver toff hat in perfect condition, placed it on his head, positioned it, and looked at them. His face looked like a baby's fist pressed against glass—soft, red, clenched, all knobs and doubt and trouble. He doffed his hat and nodded. "Percy Entwhistle. Town Drunk." He winked. "A man of refinement fallen on hard times and not reacting well. Too sensitive, really, for this world."

On these words, Percy toppled and fell forward into a perfect Pratfall, collapsing his hat. The Gimp began to clap, laughing, "You're the best, Percy. Ain't he the best?"

Percy arose and held out a hand. "Real name, Phil Rowe from Toxnard, California."

The Gimp reacted with shock. "Percy! They told you, and they told you!" He looked to Slim, eyes swimming. "He forgets. He drinks."

Percy repopped his hat and dusted himself. "We're not on the clock yet, *Timmmy.*"

Slim was shocked at the amount of hatred Percy managed to pour into that name. A distant whistle sounded. Timmy and Percy straightened. A bucket of slops hurtled lumpily from the hotel's second floor. Beneath the courthouse steps, the marmalade cat arched, hissed, spat, and whirled off. The five o'clock train whistle sounded again, closer. It was a shrill, entrepreneurial note. Slim pushed down on both guns until the belt and holsters creaked satisfyingly, squared his hat, and pivoted to face the Depot. He headed toward the tracks, in long jangly strides, spurs chipping. Timmy hastened after him, forgetting to limp for the first few yards, then floundering. "Mind if I tag along?" he said, falling back.

Percy waved after them. "Forgive me. I'm in need—" then stopped in mid-wave, pondering. "No. It's 'I require.' Yes, I'm afraid I require... Other needs... My services..." He stopped, looked at his hat with loathing, and trudged toward the Saloon, holding the hat behind him with both hands.

The train was pulling in. Slim never tired of this spectacle. The smoke from the locomotive's onion-shaped stack boiled out black and ominous, massive brakes groaned, the brass bell on the boiler swang and clanged. The odors of charred wood and singed grease reached him. White steam shot sideways from relief valves, curled around the driving wheels, and wisped from the devious chambers and piping of the inner engine organs. The engineer leaned out and turned to watch the water tower pipe swing down to hover over the reserve boiler, where the fireman waited, having knocked off the boiler cap. The engineer nodded, and the water descended in a focused, useful torrent.

Slim sighed. Way too much competence and drama for this town.

There was more. Down the steps from the first Pullman car two resplendent figures stepped lightly. The first, a solid man in fringed buckskins, Appaloosa boots, and sombrero, paused on the second step and smiled, until the lowering sun glinted on his gold-framed tooth. His companion, a slender woman in beaded denim with hammered silver and turquoise gauntlets, looked and grimaced at the town. She lifted her hat, exposing a violent shock of red hair, then turned to reboard the train. The man in the sombrero grasped her sleeve and gently turned her round.

"Calmaté, Sonrisa," the solid man said. Slim had worked with them many times before, Miguel Sands and Sonrisa "Smiley" Callahan. Miguel was the better-known. Bosses throughout the West knew enough to hire him when a crucial bit of authenticity was needed. His business cards said, simply: Miguel Sands—*Gravitas*. Smiley wasn't as well-known, but bosses who appreciated true reflexive violence with an overlay of wit and intelligence paid extra for Callahan. A few lawsuits had followed, but nothing so far that insurance couldn't cover.

As Miguel, clutching Sonrisa's arm, dropped to the platform, Timmy the Gimp mustered himself, his shoulders pumped around his ears. "*Messicans*," Timmy hissed. Miguel turned, loosing Smiley's arm. Slim had seen this before, but he always marveled. Miguel could play ages thirty to seventy, five feet four to six feet six, simply by gesture and nuance. Now he played it large, and his voice swelled as well. "*New* Mexicans," Miguel said. His voice was cultured and crisp, which made sense since he had spent years teaching elocution in New England prep schools before turning to a life of crime. "New Mexicans," he repeated, "from New Mexico. The land of enchantment that *you* will never know. Certainly a better state than this state of... Disarray."

His pause was measured and pearly, more devastating than the spoken words, and the pause was also accompanied by a dismissive flick of his hand toward the town. Timmy would have crumpled even if Sonrisa hadn't shot him. Sonrisa never spoke but thoughtfully aimed and grazed the Gimp in his other good leg. The Gimp stayed in character, arcing as he flew through the air, a move guaranteed to please the bosses. Slim stepped up. "Howdy Mig," he said, "Smiley. Glad to see yore temper ain't lengthened any."

The three stepped off the platform, arrayed themselves equally across the span of the street, and prepared for the long stroll to the Bank. They matched strides as they had done many times before. Sometimes it was the hike to the Fort, sometimes the saunter to the Corral outside of town; once they'd split up and sidled down alleys after the Marshall. Slim always enjoyed the walk. Walking was one of his best moves. He stood out because of his height and stride. Woody Strode was the only man, Slim reckoned, who could outstride him, and hell, that made sense, the man's name was Strode.

As they neared the Saloon, Slim spotted a rifle barrel edging out of the corner window on the second floor of the hotel. "I got it," Miguel said.

He fired across his chest without breaking stride, and the rifle barrel kicked up and fell backward. The shooter fired as he fell, and the bullets sailed harmlessly skyward, but oddly, each bullet ricocheted, or at least made that noise, a peculiar keening whine that lingered.

They looked at each other. "Oh Jesús," Smiley said. "Eye-tal-ians." She spat. "You think you're going to do a movie, and you end up in a goddamn film."

They hitched up and kept going. As they reached the first cross street, they got caught in a crossfire, bullets zinging in from both sides. "Angry bees!" Smiley chortled. She fired back and laughed. "A regular fusillade!"

The sulfurous odor of black powder blanks gathered in Slim's nostrils and made him smile. He fired without aiming, a lateral spray, and Miguel reloaded. While Miguel was covering the out-of-bullets Slim, the fusillade stopped. Cut off.

There was an acoustical click and then the augmented voice

of God. "Go down." They looked at each other.

"Who?" Slim mouthed.

"Slim," God intoned. "Idaho Slim goes down."

Slim, baffled, felt for his pocket Bible. He folded it back and checked the verse. It didn't say anything about him going down. He held up the Bible in mute appeal.

"Did you get the new sides?" God asked. "The gold sheets?"

"We're dead," Smiley said to Slim. "Or at least you are."

God spoke once more, this time to the Crew. "More Sweat! More Dust!" Spray bottles beaded them, wind increased, bringing dust and tumbleweeds.

They backed up until they were north of the intersection and then charged south, into the renewed fusillade. Slim threw up his arms, spun, and skidded beautifully to a stop on his back.

"I'm shot," Slim cried.

There was a long moment of hush, then again the acoustical click and the augmented voice of God. "You're dead."

Miguel knelt beside him, shading him with the Appaloosa sombrero. Slim was touched. Miguel was balding; Slim knew what a gesture it was for him to take off his sombrero. "Sorry, pard," Miguel said. "I heard some rumors 'round the chuck wagon. We got a first-time God on this one. Advertising, music videos, now the vision thing. Same old story. Behind schedule. Over budget. I guess they wrote you out."

Smiley spat. "Least they didn't build a goddamn roller rink."

Slim snorted, remembering that shoot.

Slim beckoned Miguel closer and whispered. Miguel nodded and stood up. He was playing for the bleachers now. His perfectly enunciated voice swelled and rolled out, "How could they shoot......... *Silent Slim!*"

It was everything Slim had hoped for.

Smiley Callahan smiled venomously. "Don't you worry, pardner. I'll kill 'em all."

Slim faded.

– LIMBO TIME –

(2008)

LIMBO TIME

(2008)

W E'RE SWAPPING STORIES ABOUT SUITS. SUITS
or Execs are the terms even beginning screenwriters
use to describe the executive class that abuses us—lawyers and
MBAs who have never made a movie but might have read McKee's *Story Structure*, maybe even attended a seminar or two,
which entitles them to provide notes, suggestions, always with
the weight of consensus.

My contribution is an actual classic line, from a junior Exec
at Universal. When I asked what he thought of my horror script,
which he had just finished, he replied, "I don't know. I'm the only
one who's read it."

Jaime's anecdote is a little more savage, going back to the
1988 strike when residuals were a major issue. A Warner's VP
framed the argument this way: "So should I tip my plumber every time I take a shit?"

Oscar, as always, tops us all. He has the virtue of age. He lived
through the era of proud banality that blinkered critics called
the golden age of television.

Oscar once worked on a show that lasted only one season
but remains legendary in the annals of bad television, *My
Mother the Car*. The premise of the show is that the overbearing
mother of a milquetoast lawyer dies unexpectedly, then returns

to earth inhabiting the spirit of an antique car. The voice of the mother was the acerbic Ann Sothern; Jerry Van Dyke plays her wishy-washy son; and the car is a 1928 Porter-Stanhope. Jerry visits a used car lot in search of a station wagon; his mother—the Porter—calls out to him, and he buys her on the spot. No network censors seemed to be bothered by the oedipal overtones of this transaction, so Jerry climbs inside Mom, hits her throttle, and drives her home.

Oscar described to us the day an executive nephew arrived in the writers' room in a semi-froth. Chad Hemmings was the network liaison with the sponsor, a cheese manufacturer with Christian principles. The sponsor had watched the rough cut of the first episode and had a question, which Chad framed as a complaint.

"The sponsor wants to know," Chad asked the room, "where the mother's voice is coming from." The writers looked at each other. These were not mechanics. It was a car. It was a disembodied voice. Vaguely, it seemed to them, from the region of the trunk, when Jerry first hears it. Once he's in the car, his mother's voice seems to be next to him. They really hadn't thought it through.

"What do you mean?" Oscar ventured.

Chad opened his mouth in a perfect O, pointed a forefinger to it, and said, "When I talk, my voice comes from my mouth. Where does the car's voice come from? The sponsor is a big car guy. He's also very Christian. He wants to know. Where is Mom's voice coming from?"

Oscar, after admitting he wasn't a big car guy, suggested, "Maybe the tailpipe?"

Chad pounced. "You idiots! That's what the sponsor was afraid of. You're telling us that the mother is talking out of her ass? You know what comes out of a car's tailpipe? Waste material. I need an answer."

Milton, the most junior writer, and also, like Chad, a nephew, made a stab. "Well, it should be obvious. She talks out of the carburetor. That's her mouth."

"No, no, no. That's not her mouth. That's her nose. That's how the car breathes. Are you telling me she talks through her nose?" Chad then adopted a high, fluting voice. "Like this?"

Chad cast his eyes about, Oscar tells us, in what should have been a withering glance, if his nose had not betrayed him with a glistening snot bubble that they all stared at. They waited. Chad finally saw himself in a wall mirror and fumbled for his handkerchief, which somewhat diminished his final words.

"You brainiacs need to apply a little common sense. I need an answer by tomorrow."

So Chad, Oscar tells us, slithered out the door, and then Jim, the show's creator, who hadn't said a word the whole time, started to chuckle in this irritating way that told you he'd been here before. Then Jim clapped his hands together.

"Okay, boys and girls. The Executive Wing has flown. It's LIMBO TIME. HOW LOW CAN WE GO?"

Jim made one phone call and brought in an engineer. The problem with the engineer was that he was literal. For him, the exhaust *was* the voice of the engine.

Oscar, who was not bound by literal convention, asked, "So what else makes noise in a car?"

Milton, sure he was on track this time, blurted, "The horn!"

"Limited vocabulary," Oscar said and then revealed his genius. "Let's give the car a radio."

The engineer was skeptical. "Only Chevrolets had radios in the 1920s. They cost almost as much as the car and they were huge."

"The car is from the 1920s," Oscar said. "The show takes place now. Nineteen sixty-five. The mother is an upgrade. Why can't there be other upgrades?" Television logic.

The engineer was sent away, and what sealed the deal and Oscar's career in television was his insistence that the radio lights up whenever Mom is talking to son, a visual clue. And there's one other kicker—the radio also plays a lot of jingles devoted to a certain cheese and mayonnaise manufacturer.

The sponsor was happy. That ludicrous idea for a show, that should have died a deserved death, made it to a full season: thirty slapdash episodes marred only by one cut from network censors—a backfire in the first episode is taken out since it might be mistaken for Mom farting. Limbo Time. Writers Win.

– BAT FAT –

(2009)

BAT FAT

(2009)

"**I** GOT A GUY," JAIME RUBIN SAYS, "WHO WAS present at the creation. Graduate student. Albany. Winter of 2006. Second one into the cave."

We are parked outside Bowdler's, three faded screenwriters on a bus bench in the winter sun, waiting for noon opening, and Jaime is sketching out our latest investment opportunity. Entrepreneurs and screenwriters have similar skills: we do our research, develop a story, and sell it. Since Jaime can no longer sell his ideas in Hollywood, he tries them out on us.

Jaime is riffing on an *LA Times* story he emailed us last night. It's Jaime's favorite writer, Thomas Maugh, who specializes in science and anthropology and generates more screen treatments than any writer in town.

Maugh's latest was about a bat colony in New York that starved to death, attacked by this white fungus that made them burn calories even while hibernating. Jaime also really liked the common name given to the affliction, white-nose syndrome. Reminded him of his glory days as a staff writer on *Gimme a Break!*

Oscar Grunfeld purses his lips and pulls down on his pursed lower lip with a thumb and forefinger, which is how you know Oscar is seriously thinking. "I read that article. This sounds very much like bee colony collapse syndrome."

Jaime is incensed. "Not even close. Insects versus mammals. Eyes on the prize, Oscar. Bee colony collapse? Tragedy, yes. Dividends, no."

"Tragedy," Oscar says, and then he goes walkabout. It is his only concession to age, which we think is early '80s; a word sometimes provokes a reverie.

"One Armenian dies, a tragedy," Oscar says. "One hundred thousand Armenians die, that's a statistic. Your Joseph Stalin said that." Oscar was, when he could still afford it, a Trotskyite/ Anarcho-Syndicalist. Now he owns apartment buildings. The landed man among us. He still has hopes for humankind. For tenants, not so much.

"Eyes on the prize, Oscar. Key phrases," Jaime says. "Sedentary mammals lose weight."

"Big deal," Oscar says. "When did anyone ever see a fat bat?"

"So what's the pitch?" I ask.

"Davis, Davis, Davis," Jaime says, "this one is *so* obvious, I thought even you would get it. What is the number one, surefire, money-making program in this country?"

"Probably *American Idol* or some other halfeness"—Oscar means half-ass, but he sometimes converts to Yiddish—"reality show." He sounds bitter.

"Wrongo-Bongo," Jaime says. "Number one, all-time, anytime, guaranteed, is a weight-loss program."

"This is true," I say. "I've been doing the South Park Diet, on and off, for two years."

"Don't you mean South Beach Diet?" Oscar asks.

"Naw, I modified that one. I do South Park."

And Jaime says, "Wait for it, wait for it..."

"South Park is a low-carb, low-brow diet. You cut out bread and cuss a lot."

"Badda-boom," Jaime says and does his crashing cymbal noise. "Okay, Spielbergs"—Jaime's term for Einsteins—"and among weight-loss programs, what is the crème de la crème, the Holy Donut Grail?"

Oscar and I are not at this moment Spielbergs or even Katzenbergs. We shrug.

"A passive weight-loss program," Jaime crows. "We're Americans! If you give us a choice—take-a-pill-enjoy-an-orgasm versus have-sex-have-an-orgasm—we'll take the pill every time. The whole point with this fungus is that the fungus does the heavy lifting."

"Let me see if I've got this straight," I say. "You got a guy, a grad student, who can get you this fungus?"

"Unlimited supplies. These fungi are known as GEOMYCES"—we can actually hear and almost see the capital letters in Jaime's voice— "and all they require is cold, ideally a forty-two-to-fifty-five-degree climate, and a warm mammalian body to feed on. My guy's got a pair of yaks, 'cause they like the cold. He keeps them in a refrigerated shipping container, and twice a day he combs the fungus off them. He gets nearly eight pounds of Grade-A GEOMYCES, a day. Starter kit for the average dieter is half an ounce. Do the math. The only drawback is that GEOMYCES have to be refrigerated, which makes shipping more expensive. If the temperature gets over sixty degrees, GEOMYCES die."

"That does seem a disadvantage," Oscar says, not even bothering to pull on his lip because this is so obvious.

Jaime stands up from the bus bench. "Wrongo-bongo, déjà voom! Again, Oscar." Jaime looks like he's about to float. "That's the genius part. That means the suckers have to come to us. Or buy their own refrigerated room."

I'm catching on. "So you're going to rent a meat locker and fill it full of fat naked people and cover them with a white fungus that sucks calories out of them?"

"This reminds me," Oscar says, "of Terry Southern's novel *Flash and Filigree*."

"Fat, naked, *sedated* people, Davis, and they are going to be sedated with the finest combination of recreational and twilight drugs available, but it ain't going to be no meat locker. We're gonna run this joint like a Malibu Detox Mansion. Strictly high-end.

"I mean eventually, sure, we might fill up a frozen food plant in Vernon with the HMO and Medicare crowd, but to start with, it has to be definitely high-end. Caché equals Cash. We start with a few celebrity clients, the word gets around—we'll have to hire screeners to keep out the riffraff." Jaime is in the middle of the street by now, jabbing then pointing then punctuating with his famous floating hand diorama. In the '70s he wrote a documentary about a renowned Chinese dance troupe. The dance master taught Jaime this move, "the rolling wave," a series of languid watery gestures that give the impression that Jaime's hand disconnects and floats away from his wrist.

"I mean, suppose Elizabeth Taylor is up for a Lifetime Achievement Oscar. You give La Liz this choice: One, spend one week in a medically supervised happy coma, and you are back to your *National Velvet* weight, or two, a month and a half at the No-Fun No-drinkies Fat Farm with the hourly enema plan. Which do you think she is going to choose?

"And of course, then you get into the ancillary income. Try to imagine what *National Enquirer* would pay for photos of the naked Cleopatra? I can see the headline now: *Melons covered with mold in the cold!* I'm just so sorry that Marlon didn't wait until I could provide him with the weight-loss program he deserved. Or Orson. God I could have helped him.

"And that's just the *deserving* high end. You think I couldn't convince Paris Hilton, and that other one, the other stick figure, her friend for half-life?"

"Nicole Richie," Oscar says.

"How do you *know* that?" I ask.

"A successful writer needs to stay current."

"Yeah, that's the one. You think I couldn't convince them two geniuses that they need to lose a few ounces?"

Oscar sticks out a lip, does his Edward G. Robinson thrust-head-bob. "How you going to hang them?"

This interrupts Jaime's flow and happy surveyal of all he sees and shocks him into full rant. "Hang 'em?" Jaime says. "We don't hang 'em! Whattya talking? We got four showrooms at the Malibu Fat-Free Mansion. Different rates. We show them the four levels, outline the options, they sign the contract. We give them a comp massage, put 'em under, and roll 'em out. Once they're in Comaland, who knows whether the daily floral bouquet, tantric massage, pagan prayer-cycle, aromatherapy, Chumash sage-ceremony, or Kosher acupuncture is actually delivered. We stack 'em up like cordwood in the cold room. Why would we hang them?"

"Because, flat," Oscar says, "flat is not good. You have to turn them. There is the bed sore problem, but also, if they're flat, the fungi only have access to one side of the body. This means it takes longer for the fungi to do their job. You lose money. The GEOMYCES need a full-time all-access pass to all parts of the body, don't you agree?"

Jaime looks a little stunned, but then you can see him working it. "But not upside down," Jaime says. "They're not bats. They're fat people who usually come accompanied by high blood pressure. Upside down would kill them."

"Who said upside down?" Oscar says. "What?"

But Jaime has done what he always does: reclaimed his turf, one of his small victories, the kind that got him banned from every studio in town. "Actually," Jaime says, "I think we need to sell it as an upgrade. *The Upright Suspension in the velvet-trimmed Big Baby Bouncer*™. Yeah, this will work."

The door to Bowdler's swings open and Day Bartender Kenny Ishikawa blocks it open with a trashcan and starts pulling chairs down from tables.

"Ahh," Oscar says, "time for a libation."

Jaime takes a stand. "Are you guys with me on this? The last surefire, ground-floor opportunity of your lifetime?"

"No cash," I say.

"No enthusiasm," Oscar says. "Come, Hymie"— Jaime's preferred pronunciation—"let me invest in a libation for you."

But Jaime has talked himself up, the way he used to when he was known as one of the best pitchers in town. He is high on himself and needs no alcohol to sustain that high.

"Drawing the line here," Jaime says. "I'm going to go home. I'm going to work on my prospectus. And then I'll head for Musso's, where some real investors may still be found."

Kenny comes out to retrieve the trashcan, and as he lifts it, Jaime calls to him, "Yo, Kelsoe. Buy these losers a drink. Put it on my tab." Kenny switches hands and waves vaguely at Jaime. "Lack of commitment," Jaime says. "You see how uncommitted that was? That slack, loosey-goosey pretend wave. The problem with this country, *hahh*"—it sounds like a hairball coming up—"*hagggh*, is that lack of commitment."

"Onward," Oscar says. "Onward!" Oscar salutes, emphatically, then walks into and is absorbed by the dark recesses of Bowdler's. I follow him.

• •

W E DON'T SEE JAIME FOR A FEW WEEKS, AND when he rejoins us at Bowdler's, it is hard to gauge his attitude. He doesn't seem chastened, but he is not the inflated Jaime we saw last. The balloon didn't get popped, but maybe it lost a little volume. Jaime walks through the door, nods to Kenny, and sits at our table. He flattens his hands on the table and spreads his fingers. "Gentlemen," Jaime says, "I'll accept that libation now."

Oscar decides to torment Jaime by buying him that promised drink and not asking what happened.

Oscar, as though he is continuing an interrupted conversation, says, "Did either of you know Terry Southern? No? No? Before your time." Jaime's vodka martini with fresh ground pepper, two olives, and an onion arrives. "A wonderful train wreck waiting to happen. Incredible talent, incredibly abused." Jaime lifts and sips, and Oscar catches him mid-sip. "In case you should ever feel sorry for yourself, think of Terry Southern.

"He rewrote *The Killing* for Kubrick, no credit, almost no money, then wrote *Dr. Strangelove*, and Kubrick screwed him again, both credits and money. Southern wises up, swears off Kubrick, and then gets totally screwed on *Easy Rider*, and that vas worse because now he vas being screwed by amateurs. I mean, Kubrick is Kubrick. A worthy adversary. But when your throwaway genius is credited to a Dennis Grasshopper? It killed him."

"That's sad," Jaime interrupts. "Let me tell you another sad story ..."

But Oscar rolls on. "When he died, they went to that Grasshopper and asked for help, to keep him from a pauper's grave, and you know what that insect said? He said he didn't want to set a precedent. He said that if he had to buy funerals for all the writers he had screwed, he'd be bankrupt in a month. Fehh. It's the business we are in."

Jaime can stand it no longer. "Do you remember the last time we talked?"

Oscar tosses off his crème de menthe and slams the cordial glass down. "How can you not know Terry Southern?"

Jaime glares.

"So, Ja," Oscar says. "Tell us about the bat fat."

"It worked," Jaime says. "It actually worked. So close, but there was just this little problem with the delivery system. The geomyces"—Oscar and I both note that they are no longer capitalized—"were really good at sucking calories, but they couldn't hang on."

"Hang on?" I say.

"They slid off."

"Slid off..."

"Skin. They didn't much like smooth skin."

"Skin," Oscar says.

"The thing about bats," Jaime says, "is that they are furry little fuckers. Completely covered with hair. Which was good for the geomyces. So they could hold on. Humans are relatively hairless. Orderly opens door, one puff of air, valuable geomyces are floating up around the vents."

Jaime arrays his onion and olives on a napkin, downs the martini, and holds up the empty glass. "Yo, Kelsoe," he says. Kenny, who is charitable today, hands over a ready-made exchange martini. Oscar and I turn and stare. Kenny settles back next to the cash register and picks up his book. Today he is reading a favorite, Jean Rhys's *Wide Sargasso Sea*. Beside him are two more ready-made martinis. Kenny senses our stares and looks up. "What? At least he's trying to do something." Oscar and I are staggered. It never occurred to us that Kenny might listen to anything one of us had to say.

Jaime pops an olive, "What we figured out was it would have to be a two-step process. First step, you would have to grow hair all over your body so the geomyces would have something to cling to. That would be a deal-breaker for most women, and the depilatory factor only screwed it further. Once they'd lost the weight, full body bikini waxing. Then laser. Maybe some radiation ..."

"Ouch," Oscar says.

"Not cost-effective." Jaime pops an olive then closes with an onion and downs his second martini with a swirling flourish. Kenny again makes a gracious exchange.

"You don't seem that daunted," I say.

Jaime sips. "It set me back for a day or two, particularly because I'd found some *serious* investors, but I think it's going to work out. I sold off a half-interest to a guy who thinks he can find enough fat, hairy guys to make a profit."

"No shortage there," I say. "Start with the Weinsteins, work your way up to Rudin."

"You should have started with Coppola," Oscar tells me. "The obvious choice if you weren't such an anti-Semite."

Jaime waits for us to settle down, like that genius fifth-grade teacher you had who knew exactly how to read a class. We settle.

"I think I'll be okay," Jaime says. "Once you immerse yourself in the world of weight loss, you learn that there are myriad ways to skin that particular cat." A gleam ignites in the depths of Jaime's eyes. "How much do you know about tapeworms?"

Oscar and I glance at each other. "Obviously not enough," I say.

Jaime expands, once again, to full entrepreneurial size. "In many ways, tapeworms are the ideal diet aid. No restriction on caloric intake, no need for unwanted exercise. Their only drawback is that when tapeworms reach maximum size, thirty meters, they become injurious to their hosts, and if they should reproduce, the fuckers can kill you.

"But I think there is a workable solution. All we need is tapeworms with a shelf-life." We wait for it. "I gotta guy," Jaime says, "a Doctor Musharaff, Mushariff, one of those, who can deliver to me irradiated tapeworms of any size, in any quantity. These are prime Pakistani tapeworms, not those feeble two-inchers the Indonesians are flooding the market with.

"Great appetites. Because they are irradiated, they are sterile and will die peacefully within six months, once they have achieved our goals. We can predict a thirty-pound weight loss in that period, but of course you can always upgrade, buy more than one if you want to lose more or lose it faster. And of course, the vacuum enemas would be complimentary."

"Irradiated tapeworms," Oscar says slowly. "I must say, Jaime Rubin, you are a man with courage and vision."

"I know it," Jaime says grandly, his famous floating hand gesture encompasses us, the room, and Kenny, who rises involuntarily, reaching for that third martini. "I wouldn't be where I am today without that vision."

It is the wisdom of the room, one I have learned to trust. We reverse here the process that the chambered nautilus uses to create its world. The nautilus begins with a microscopic chamber and builds spiraling outward, larger and larger, sealed and airtight rooms. We three, and our tender, Kenny, have retreated, year after year from a lifetime of education, work, struggle, humiliation, and employment to this small place where we are secure and well entertained, and Jaime trusts that he edifies and amuses. It is a style and a comfort. A small chamber with music we agree on.

– "LA NOVIA" –

FROM THE JOURNALS
OF DALE DAVIS

(1987)

"LA NOVIA"

FROM THE JOURNALS
OF DALE DAVIS

(1987)

O N MY LAST DAY IN NICARAGUA, I WAS TAKEN
to Niquinohomo, the birthplace of Augusto Sandino.
There I was to meet La Novia de Sandino, Sandino's fiancée. Maria Soledad was her name. She was a tall, dignified woman in her
eighties. Her hair looked like cotton fluff around her walnut-col-
ored face. I was introduced, "El es Señor Dale Davis de Estados
Unidos." She was introduced as La Novia de Sandino, and her
head went up and her shoulders stiffened at the phrase. On the
road to León I had questioned my guide, a Sandinista press officer. Dionisio was a small, stocky man with a tailored uniform
and an elaborate moustache. I thought I'd misunderstood, You
mean the widow of Sandino? No, he explained carefully, she was
the fiancée. They had never married. They had been engaged a
year, then Sandino had gone to Mexico for work. When he returned to Niquinohomo, he'd killed a Conservative Party member in a duel and had to flee. After that, he'd begun the fight
against the Los Yanquis and had gone to the mountains.

That was six years, and when the war was over and the Norteamericanos had gone home, they had eight months together. The wedding was to be in March 1934. Then the Somocistas had assassinated him. She had been Sandino's fiancée now for sixty years. She was not much of a talker; she volunteered little. She said that Sandino had been a good man, a strong man, but gentle and respectful, and after he died, she knew that she would never marry. She was sorry that she had no children, but no other man had ever interested her.

She showed us a photograph of herself—an open-faced woman of twenty with glossy hair—and Sandino, a slender, handsome man in a campaign hat. They stood in front of a Malinché tree that was in bloom. On the walls of her kitchen there were more pictures, but only of her, in front of the same Malinché tree. In succeeding years, the tree had grown, and she had shrunk. The recent pictures were in color, and you could see the beautiful orange blossoms. She said she still missed him.

And that was the interview. She shook my hand and Dionisio's hand, sat down, and waited for us to leave. It was about four o'clock when we pushed the Toyota around—the reverse gear was out—and headed back. It was a little more than twenty miles back to Managua. Granada, the old Conservative capital, was ten miles away to the east. León, the old Liberal capital, was about seventy miles from Granada. Managua was the compromise capital, like Sacramento in California, situated between two opposed cities. Within that seventy-mile span, smaller than the Los Angeles basin, Augusto Sandino had chased, or had been chased by, US Marines for six years.

Dionisio was quiet in the car, and I sensed that the visit to Sandino's fiancée had affected him deeply. I welcomed his silence. For two days he had lectured and entertained me nonstop. Dionisio was the third stop for me. After the plug was pulled on the picture, the studio's line producer, Sid Newman, held on to me for two days, trying

to convince me to sign waivers. He finally handed me off to his ad-
min assistant, Kevin. Kevin couldn't convince me either; when it was
time for him to fly out, they called in their last governmental favor,
handing me off to the Sandinistas, who selected Dionisio because he
clearly didn't have anything else to do.

Dionisio had no idea who I was; he didn't know that a North
American studio had been attempting a movie in Nicaragua. He
didn't know the attempt had failed. He was told I was a writer.
He assumed I was a journalist.

He believed strongly in the revolution, but like everyone else
you met in Nicaragua below ministerial rank, he had a family to
feed. He had dealt with North Americans before and knew that
the subtle emotional interplay of Nicaraguan commerce did not
register with us. The wrinkle of a nose, which would mean vol-
umes to a countryman, was a lost signal. We lacked the radar. He
made it clear on our first day that his revolutionary beliefs did
not rule out gas, meals, or appropriate gifts. Dionisio's favorite
expression began with the tilt of an eyebrow, then a slowly tilting
smile and a waggling finger: "All-expense account, no?" Now he
was clearly brooding.

I suggested we stop for dinner, and he pulled in at *El Volcan*,
a few miles from Managua. The restaurant was a big square room
with high ceilings that was open at one end. It felt like a small
airplane hangar. There were more than fifty square tables, each
with a blue plastic tulip in a plastic vase. Each was covered with
a red plasticized cloth and surrounded by four ornately carved
ladder-back chairs. A waiter came out from the shadows near the
kitchen and gestured to us that we could sit where we liked. We
were the only customers. He carried menus bound in red leather,
but he did not offer them. We ordered rum and asked if we could
eat. The waiter put the menus behind his back; he said he would
check with the kitchen and see what was available.

He returned with a kerosene lamp, a bottle of white Flor de

Caña, ice, limes, glasses, and two small pitchers of fruit juices—papaya and guava, it looked like. He lifted the chimney of the lamp and lit the wick with the ceremony and drama that all waiters provide when they have a match in their hands. His white hair and cheekbones flared in the flame. Some beef was available, he told us. Chicken also was available, but if we wanted chicken, we would both have to order it. The owner wouldn't kill a chicken for one. We ordered the beef. Dionisio came to life after his second rum. He mustered a smile. "When do you go back to Los Angeles?" he asked.

"Tomorrow," I said.

"And what is your impression of our country?"

The question seemed official. I gave the official answer. "I like the people. I'm sorry the economy is so bad. I'm sorry to see the suffering this has caused."

Dionisio tossed the last inch of his rum/papaya and poured another, heavy on the rum. "Ah yes, the famous embargo. Will you write about that?"

I nodded. He nodded. The party line, which Dionisio had hammered home the last two days, was that the embargo and the cost of the war had wrecked a flourishing economy. I thought there were other factors, but it wasn't worth arguing about tonight. Dionisio leaned forward into the glow of the table lamp. His eyes and his mustache shone in the buttery light. "I have a favor," he said.

This could mean anything from help with a visa to sponsorship to an exchange of córdobas for dollars. I felt myself stiffening, and I felt him sense it. "No," he said. "No, it's a small favor." He held out a small plastic and rubber part. It looked like plumbing. The plastic tabs were cracked, mended, cracked again, and the rubber seal was frayed. "It's a North American toilet," he said. "I can't get the parts."

"Of course," I said and took the part.

"It's a small thing," he said, "but it runs night and day. It wakes me up. Now I have a cork stuck in the pipe. My wife is embarrassed because she has to ask me to flush. This is the number." He handed me a slip of paper with the toilet make, American Standard, and the serial number. He brought out some bills from his shirt pocket, 500 and 1,000 córdoba notes.

"No, no," I said. "My treat. Your money's no good."

He laughed then, a short, barking laugh, looking at the money in his fist. "It's true," he said. "Exactamente." The córdoba had been devalued the previous day. The official rate of exchange was now 7,500 córdobas to the dollar. The black-market rate was 10–12,000, and near the Honduran border it was over 40,000.

He held one of the 500 córdoba notes up on my side of the lamp. "Has anyone shown you this?" Everyone had shown me this, from the first day I'd arrived, but I said, "What?"

"The ghost of Sandino," Dionisio said. With the light shining through the bill, I could see the watermark: General A. C. Sandino in his big hat.

He put the bill flat on the table so that I was looking down at the face of Ruben Dario, Nicaragua's famous poet. Dionisio finished his drink and rattled the ice cubes. He poured more rum— he was drinking it straight now—and topped off my drink. "My brother used to say, 'If you can't hear the ice, you're drinking too slow.'" His forefinger tapped the bill. "Do you know Dario?"

"Poquito," I said. "A little. The elegies."

"Nobody does," Dionisio said. He was drunk now. His brow glistened, and his mouth hung open. "They worship that mouse, Cardenal. Do you know, they say he joined the church because his mother had a vision? Cardinal Cardenal!

"As a politician, he is admirable. As a poet he is an insect. But he *is* read. Not Dario, he is too difficult." Dionisio slammed his fist down on the table. "Where is our dinner?" The waiter, who rose as the silverware jumped and clattered, wafted over. He leaned close to Dionisio's ear, turning away from me, whispered, then backed away.

Dionisio winked and poured more rum. "It seems they have to catch the calf. Or the meat was frozen. Or it is a stew and requires more time. Pick your answer. Whichever one you choose is closer to the truth than what that maricón told me."

He topped off my glass again, spilling rum into the saucer, and then lifted his glass in a toast: "North American toilets!" He swallowed his drink and shuddered.

I called the waiter over, "Por favor. Hay antojitos? Hors d'oeuvres?" He looked mournful, shrugged, and went to the kitchen. He returned with a plate of chopped carrots, a small tomato, and more limes. By then Dionisio had fixed himself another drink. He handed the empty bottle to the waiter. "Un otro."

He bent to sip from his brimming glass, then leaned into the lamplight to wink at me. "Think of it," he said. "La Novia. Eighty years a virgin. To honor a good man. Not like your Jackie-O, no?" He winked again.

I offered him the tomato and carrots, but he waved them away. He was quite drunk by now. He angled his chair to stare at the waiter in the shadows and then turned back to me. "He was embarrassed. He had to lie because of you." He twirled the ice in his glass and sucked his finger. "It is, of course, the national response. A Norteamericano visits us, of course we're embarrassed. Does it offend you that I refer to North America? To the possibility of more than one America?"

I shook my head. "No."

Dionisio closed one eye to focus on me. "All Central America is a North American toilet. You flush. We swim in the whirlpool." He shifted eyes and focused on the 500 córdoba note in front of me. "What kind of country puts a poet on its money?"

He reached for the bill and knocked over his drink. As it pooled and flowed to spill over the edge of the table, Dionisio stood and walked away. He stopped at the open end of the room, steadied himself with a hand on a chair, and looked out at the rows of stunted banana trees beyond a field of sugar cane stubble. The charred stubs and broken stalks of the cane glinted like obsidian in the lowering sun.

The waiter came and mopped Dionisio's side of the table. He put down a fresh placemat and silverware and made a drink from a new bottle of rum. He vanished as Dionisio wobbled back toward our table.

Dionisio's knees hit the second, third, and fourth chairs in his path. It was like watching a hurdler. Once the first hurdle was tipped, the next and the next would topple until the runner adjusted stride. Dionisio adjusted by stopping. He stood very still, one hand on a chair, one on a table, and you could feel him gathering himself. He straightened and walked steadily toward me, stopping at his chair, his hands resting lightly on the back. "How can you kill us?" Dionisio said. "When you don't know who we are?"

I had heard the line months before, in Los Angeles—it was a quote from a *Barricada* columnist, but even if it had been fresh, there was no answer. Orwell had the answer; he would have said, "But that's the only way we *can* kill you." But even Orwell wouldn't have answered tonight.

Dionisio gave up on me. He walked on, to the entrance, and went outside. After a few minutes I went there myself. The Toyota was gone.

As I returned to the table, the waiter swung out from the kitchen, bearing two plates aloft. He set them on the table with a small flourish—a half a roasted chicken was on each plate, garnished with carrots and tomatoes.

"There was a problem with the beef," he said, "which we could not resolve."

"I need a taxi," I told him, "to go to Managua." He said there would be no problem.

"Would you like to dine with me?" I asked.

"No," he told me. "Gracias. I have already eaten." He put a napkin over the other plate and went to call the taxi.

The chicken smelled fine, but I wasn't hungry. By the time the taxi arrived, I'd put a napkin over my own plate. The table looked decidedly funereal. I picked up the plumbing part and put it in my pocket, then went to the desk near the entrance.

The waiter handed me the bill and waited while I unlatched my briefcase. The cook, a heavy woman dressed in white with a child attached to her knees, had come out from the kitchen to watch. The taxi driver loitered discreetly in the doorway. I brought out a six-inch stack of córdobas.

The bill was itemized. The ice was more expensive than the rum, and the tip was included. It came to 106,000 córdobas. Or fourteen dollars North American. I began counting off from the stack and thought of my colleague, who had papered two sides of her home office—floor to ceiling—with Nicaraguan currency. It was cheaper, she said, than wallpaper. I added 15,000 for the waiter, who nodded thanks but did not bow. It was clear that he had hoped for dollars.

– DESPERATE TIMES, DESPERATE CRIMES –

(2010)

DESPERATE TIMES, DESPERATE CRIMES

(2010)

———————

ESPERATE TIMES CALL FOR DESPERATE MEASURES. Guy Fawkes said that, and so did Esmerelda, Gustavo's daughter, when I went to visit him at the hospital. Gustavo is my landlord of seven years, owner of the place I landed once the scripts went un-optioned and the residuals dried up, an eight-bungalow court on the fringe of Culver City.

What Esmerelda actually said was, "I'm sorry, but we got to bump the rent."

I was the one who said the thing about desperate times.

Once Gustavo's lung cancer put him—a man who never smoked and wouldn't rent to smokers—in the hospital, Esmerelda got a look at the books. Turned out Gus had been carrying me for most of those seven years. He'd appointed me court manager five years ago, a nebulous title with almost nonexistent duties. I was paying $750 a month for a $1,200 mock witch's cottage. Property values and taxes in Culver City were spiraling upward. Both Sony and Culver Studios were expanding, buying up blocks of formerly distressed properties.

Outside Gus's room, Esmerelda said she would have to bump everybody else's rent to $1,500 just to stay even. My rent would go up to $1,200, and future hikes were probable. I knew that was fair, and I told Esmerelda so. She got a little teary. "I hated to tell you. My dad never would."

I went back in to say goodbye to Gus, but he was asleep. The gray stubble on his cheeks was now darker than the crepey white pallor of his skin, and I understood that this might really be goodbye.

Gus was one of the last links to my apotheosis, my one directorial credit, *Head-In-Bag*, the punk version of Sam Peckinpah's *Bring Me the Head of Alfredo Garcia*. Filmed in Nicaragua in 1987 and never shown. The high point of my career. Ham in a can.

Gus had been the lead set carpenter on the shoot. Sixteen years later, when he met me at the court to show me the vacancy, he smiled at me quizzically. "Dale Davis. I don't know if you remember me..."

"Vividly," I said. "You were the guy who let me know the local actors were stealing plywood." And who could blame them? A four-by-eight sheet of plywood during the Reagan embargo was worth three months' wages. Then I had to ask the obligatory question: "Was I an asshole?" It is hard to remember, on long-ago shoots, how well you handled the pressure.

"Naw, you were okay. No more of an asshole than usual. Actually, that was one of my favorite shoots." He winked. "And it wasn't spoiled by bad reviews." Later he showed me a photo he'd taken of our cast and crew party on the beach at San Juan del Sur. I looked like Carmen Miranda, buried in sand up to my neck, surrounded by a mound of tropical fruit, drunk and happy even though they'd shut us down.

And now that time of moderate ambitions and low rent was closing fast. It was that time. As the Buddhists say, if you don't like the answer, change the question. As my credits age, the competition for crap jobs—teaching, writing or rewriting student scripts, under-the-table script doctoring—is intensifying as other writers age out and into my marginal world. Doors no longer get slammed on me. They never open. I am in trouble and even with a long ladder and a periscope, I can't see a way out of the ditch I've dug myself into.

I went back to the apartment and broke into my savings account—my last two Bukowski rarities, hardback signed first editions of *Post Office* and *Love Is a Dog From Hell*. That one also has a little dog doodle. They weren't hard to find, turned backward on the shelf so that I wouldn't have to discuss the literary merits of that gaseous old windbag with any guests.

Together they should bring something close to three, maybe three and a half grand at Barricade Books on Las Palmas, a Bukowski shrine run by Sol "Reb" Haverstein who thinks that when you look in the dictionary under *curmudgeon* his picture should appear.

It's the perfect pairing for a man like myself who uses the principle of Occam's Razor to justify sloth. The bookstore is two blocks from Bowdler's, the bar where I have to be that afternoon for my usual Wednesday afternoon meeting with my comrades in obsolescence, Jaime Rubin and Oscar Grunfeld.

· ·

O SCAR, AS ALWAYS, IS PUNCTUAL. THE FIRST OF his course of liqueurs is before him. A small snifter of Cointreau. Kenny looks up from his book as I open the door and rings the brass bell next to the cash register.

Kenny has my usual, brandy and soda, in front of me as I slide into the booth. "Jaime will be slightly delayed," Oscar says. "A late night of research for a new project. And how are you?" With Oscar the question is genuine. It's been a week since we've seen each other. He's doing well and wants the same for me.

"Well," I lie, "one of my former students got a job at Parallax and is circulating one of my scripts under an assumed name. It's made the second cut."

Unfortunately, Oscar has spied the bubble-wrapped Bukowski in my satchel. "Oh Dale, no. You're not going to see Sol. Do you need some money?"

"It's not that. I'm just tired of looking at them, and the market is high right now. "

"Not for you. Not with Sol. You know what a putz he is, and he knows you hate Bukowski. I know the guy. I've had this conversation. He wasn't at the party, but he heard about it."

I don't know what Oscar is talking about but can only assume this was back when I could still afford friends who could afford cocaine.

Oscar looks at me imploringly. "Do you need some money? Please. Let me help."

I can't do it. Not yet. The books will hold me a month or two. "I'm all right, Oscar. Really. Lotta flies in the ointment."

I am saved by distraction. The front door cracks open, the white sunlight of Los Angeles streaks in, and Jaime Rubin slides through. Kenny rings his bell and calls out, "We now have a minyan. Bozoes at Bowdler's!"

Oscar and I lift our glasses and Jaime intones, "Yo, Kelsoe. The usual."

Kenny has Jaime's martini ready to shake. He pours, lifts the pepper grinder above the glass, and cranks. Presents.

Jaime takes a sip, a brief shudder, a nod. Another sip, a dip and turn, and he bows in Kenny's general direction. Kenny, the only reader among us without an agenda, has returned to his paperback under the penlight next to the cash register, Marilynne Robinson's *Lila*.

Jaime eases into our booth, sips again, and unclenches. "Another long night of research."

Oscar and I lift supplicatory palms. Research has been mentioned; next comes the pitch. Jaime sips and gazes at Oscar. "You've had a long, good life. Forget what your tenants say about you. How much longer would you like to live?"

Oscar doesn't have to consider. "Long enough to see Kissinger in jail and Netanyahu fail."

"So," Jaime says, "a few more years?"

"If it takes that," Oscar replies. "But I would leave tomorrow if those conditions were met."

"I would say that may take a few more years. And if you have to persist, here is an alternative to consider." Jaime puts his martini glass definitively on the table. The gathering commences. We've witnessed this moment before but can't look away. Even Kenny puts down his paperback and switches off the penlight. Jaime seems to swell. You can sense the churn of ideas; a slow, spreading smile takes over his face. You can almost hear a distant calliope.

"Okay, boys and girls. I'm not going to give you the full prospectus here. We're not going to nail down the names and dates. You're not going to get the footnotes, just the sizzle. The steak is for genuine investors."

Jaime's eyebrows do a little doo-dah dance. He's approaching full twinkle. "Nineteen fifty-four. A guy named Clive McCray at Cornell sews together an old rat and a young rat. This is not a transfusion. This is linkage, parabiosis, constant flow, old rat blood cycles into young rat, comes back refreshed, new outlook on life. Young rat, not so good, but manageable. He gets a few extra pellets for his trouble, doesn't kill the old fuck he's sewn onto. Extrapolate!"

Oscar seems lost in thought, which means I have to step up. "Fountain of Youth time?"

"No, no, no, and no," Jaime says, eyebrows dancing in rhythm. It's like watching Groucho Marx and Frida Kahlo ending a tango. "Fountain of Youth is gulp, swallow, I feel better. That's transfusion. The real cure takes commitment. Old body joined surgically to young body—not a temporary boost. We are talking transubstantiation. The three T's: time, together, tethered.

"Later studies confirm the earlier findings—2004 Harvard med, stem cells revived. Stanford, 2006, brain functions improved. Nice spa visit for old rats. For young rats, not such a great deal. But again, in the lab, controlled circumstances. Let's take it outside the lab. Out on the street, how do you get young rats to cooperate?"

"More pellets?" I suggest.

"But we're not in the lab anymore. Who wants pellets? We need volunteers."

Sadly, I still like to provoke Jaime. "Is this the homeless solution?"

"Not good donors. My clients, the rich, the elderly, are going to want pristine, healthy blood."

Oscar comes to life, head tilted merrily, hand raised. "Unless they want to get younger, healthier, and *high*!" Terry Southern, *Blood of a Wig*. Oscar trots out his heroes with regularity. Terry Southern is one, and we know the story he cites, jaded heads in NYC seeking the ultimate high, pints of paranoid schizophrenic blood fresh from the locked wards at Bellevue. Jaime ignores him.

He looks at me. "When did you graduate from college?" He knows the answer.

"Nineteen seventy-eight," I reply. "UC Santa Cruz. Go Banana Slugs."

"And how much did you accrue in student loans?"

"Didn't have to. We paid no tuition. That was your birthright as a Californian. A free college education."

"Not anymore. The average graduate of what used to be a state university now takes six years to complete their studies and accrues 100K in debt. You graduate with a degree in any of the liberal arts—English, Gender Studies, Anthropology—what we now call pre-law, you're looking at twenty years of payments.

"So, you now have something we haven't had for two centuries—indentured servants. You think a few of the indentured wouldn't jump at the chance of a way out? Here's the pitch. You are sutured to an ancient billionaire—or maybe not such an ancient given the way Silicon Valley is trending—medically monitored, given the best of care for six months, and your student loans are forgiven. Not that different from a surrogate pregnancy with a lot happier ending."

Oscar stirs. "I remember that movie."

Jaime clasps his head. "Whattya talking? This is an up-to-date idea. The *New York Times* article was only last week." Jaime whips out his clipping, "Young Blood May Hold Key to Reversing Aging," by one of his favorite sources, Carl Zimmer.

Oscar has focused, which is daunting. "No!" he thunders, "I remember that movie."

Jaime is frosty. "What does this have to do with my *very* original idea of blood transubstantiation?"

"It's an old story," Oscar says. "Rich sewn to poor. It's been done. Nineteen seventy-two. *The Thing with Two Heads*. Ray Milland's head sewn to Rosey Grier's shoulder. Cheek to cheek. Milland is a racist. They hate each other. Terrible movie. The same year Milland did *Frogs*, another terrible movie. The man who won an Oscar for *Lost Weekend*. He said he needed the money. I think he just hated staying home."

Jaime has given up his pitch. I watch him deflate—first it's a pinhole, then it's a blowout, eyes and eyebrows rolling like snakes on a griddle.

Oscar continues our history lesson. "He'd have to face a summer shoot featuring fifteen car crashes and an ape with two heads, all written by a schlockmeister like Lee Frost. He must have hated staying at home."

"You ever work with him?"

Oscar looks provoked. "Lee Frost? Never. This is the man who invented Nazisploitation with *Love Camp 7.* Strictly Grindhouse and B-minus drive-in. *Chrome and Hot Leather* and *Chain Gang Women* were some of his better titles. They'd throw in beaver shots for the European market."

Jaime has left us. Out the back door for once, not even staging his exit.

"Tell me more about *The Thing with Two Heads.*" Something in the description intrigued me.

"It was actually a great idea. Where they stole it from, I don't know. Milland plays this world-renowned surgeon, a genius at transplants, dying of cancer. His body is wasting, his brain is full of ideas. He knows a cure is on the way, but he can't wait. He's pre-cryogenic. He's not Walt Disney—no head in the ice. He decides the solution is his head on a healthy body. He has a friend who is head of all the prisons in the state. A healthy prisoner, plucked from death row will be the donor.

"Those about to be executed are told that it is an experimental medical program, no more than that. Sounds like a good deal for both sides. Both sides are disappointed. The Rosey Grier character because he has a nasty head next to him and the good doctor, Milland, because he somehow forgot that 90 percent of the prisoners on death row are Black, and he happens to be a Mississippi racist.

"As I said, the situation is intriguing, but the schlockmeister side takes over, and from there you have a half-hour motorcycle chase with fifteen car crashes. Downhill from there. Such a waste of a good idea." Oscar finishes his Cointreau and raises the next liqueur in the set, crème de menthe in a tulip stem glass, in a toast: "Lee Frost, *Yimakh shmoy zol er vern!*" It sounds like he's gargling razor blades.

"And in English," I say.

"There is no suitable translation. 'May his name and memory

be erased' is as close as you can come."

I remain intrigued. I'm not sure why. But the itch at the base of my skull, the one that every writer knows, tells me that I am on the hunt. "It *is* a good idea," I tell Oscar. "Certainly, a better one than *Guess Who's Coming to Dinner?* I wonder who holds the rights?"

"The audience is there," Oscar says. He's halfway through the crème de menthe and enjoying himself. "Of course, if you really want to mix your metaphors and your crowds, combine *The Thing with Two Heads* and *Blood of a Wig*. Put George Burns's head on Dennis Rodman's shoulders." He cackles.

I take my leave. It's four o'clock, and Barricade Books is about to open. I walk the long way down Hollywood Boulevard, past the Supply Sergeant, home to all things camouflage and war surplus, past Book City, where color-coded books are sold by the shelf-foot to set designers, past Musso-Frank's, and then turn toward Las Palmas.

Oscar is a little wrong. I don't *hate* Bukowski. I think he's written one and two-thirds good books, *Ham and Rye* and *Post Office*. I also think he's sloppy, repetitive, lazy, repetitive, sentimental beyond Hallmark, did I mention repetitive, and he has a problem with women. Now, that's an odd take for a man like myself, who has been married four times, but my problems are the opposite. Bukowski doesn't like them very much.

Barricade Books keeps odd hours—four to midnight, Wednesdays to Sundays—geared to the store's primary source of income: drunken screenwriters, actors, directors, producers, and executives drifting down from Musso-Frank's a block away, looking for overpriced books and broadsides by the drunken poet they think they'd like to be, Charles Bukowski.

The curator, Sol "Reb" Haverstein, a paunchy man in a neon yellow track suit, blocks the doorway as I approach and issues his customary greeting. "Whattya want? You buying or selling?"

Apparently, this bit of local color thrills the yokels from Musso's. Reb's nimbus of hair is larger and whiter than last time and so is the puff of chest hair protruding from his unzipped decolletage. "In the past I've bought," I tell him. "Some nice Baudelaire. Today I'm selling. Bukowski."

He steps aside. The front window has a pull-down deep red glassine shade that blocks ultra-violet rays, preventing harm to valuable books and prints, but it also creates a weird red glow. It feels like you're inside a glass factory, without the heat.

The shop has become even more of a shrine to Bukowski than I remember. But then, of course, Bukowski is dead. Jesús, I think I just remembered the party Oscar was talking about. I hand over the bubble-wrapped books to Reb and he takes them to his desk, brings out a large square magnifying glass.

Nineteen ninety-five. First anniversary of Bukowski's death and two of my aforementioned cokehead friends, huge Bukowski fans, drag me along to a memorial party and reading in Venice. After an hour and a half of drunken blubbering, recitations, competitive memories, and homages, I couldn't stand it. I took my place at the podium.

I looked down at the sea of open-mouthed expectant faces and opened my copy of *Fires*. "I'm Dale Davis. I am going to read what is *by far* the *best* Bukowski poem ever written." Pause. "You Don't Know What Love Is. An Evening With Charles Bukowski." Big pause.

"By Raymond Carver."

It still doesn't register. I was two minutes in before the booing started, and it was probably three minutes before some of the bravoes rushed the stage and tried to drag me off. It took them a while. These weren't working-class louts but the usual feeble white-collar Bukowski wannabes, and I was laughing so hard I was slippery.

"These are good," Reb says. "Do you want to leave them on consignment, or do you want cash?"

"I think cash this time," I say. "I'm leaving for a location shoot in the Canaries next week, and it would be good to have a little walkaround."

"Cash. Then it will be three thousand for the two. You're sure? Consignment would be seven."

"Let's make it cash," I say.

"So, who do I make the check out to?"

"You don't have cash in hand?"

"In this neighborhood? Do I look like a fool? What's the name for the check?"

"Umm, make it out to D. D. Davis."

"These books are inscribed to Dale. Is that you?

"Just D. Davis is fine."

"Are you Dale Davis?"

It's a little like watching a roadside thermometer in fast-forward the way the flush ascends from his unzipped chest to his swollen forehead, but his movements are deliberate. Reb opens his desk and brings out a large oval stamp and pad, inks it, opens each book to Bukowski's signature and rocks it. BOGUS the stamp says. Reb signs them and hands the books to me. "Now try to sell them. Get out of my store, you insult to Buk ..." He pronounces *Buk* to rhyme with *puke*, a mark of the true believer.

Out on the street I look at the convenient trash can, but it's a gesture I can't afford. They are still first editions, worth a couple hundred each, even devalued. And they are definitely devalued. Reb is brought in to authenticate Bukowski's work; his opinion is accepted. If I can't sell them, they're great kindling for my funeral pyre, but right now other priorities. First, my friend Gyorgy, who used to work at Vidiots until he compiled the largest private collection of videos and DVDs in So Cal. If he doesn't have a copy of *The Thing with Two Heads* he'll know who does, and then my friend Shauna at CBS legal, who will track down the rights for me by Monday.

· ·

THE MOVIE IS AS BAD AS OSCAR DESCRIBED. EVEN Milland couldn't save it. At one point Rosey Grier, escaped from capture on the aforementioned stolen motorcycle, meets up with his woman. Feeling a bit horny, he suggests sex. She's put off by Milland's head, so Rosey offers to cover it with a pillowcase, but she demurs. Most viewers, if offered a pillowcase at that point, would probably accept.

The rights, it turns out, have descended to a niece, a nice woman now in her forties named Magda, who fortunately has an inflated view of Uncle Lee's artistic vision. She thinks of him as Quentin Tarantino before his time, a view I am happy to honor, particularly if it will save me a few bucks.

Magda would like to meet at Musso's to discuss, a proposal that I instantly scotch. Musso-Frank's makes Hollywood dreams expand, and I need that horizon shrunk to a thin line. We meet at Magda's for tea.

The conversation is slowed at first by my admission that I don't know Uncle Lee's full oeuvre. I've never seen *Dixie Dynamite* nor *Black Gestapo*, but I am pretty convincing on the virtues of *The Thing with Two Heads*, as a lesson in race relations the country needs now! The asterisk that I add is the gradual effect that sharing blood with a Black man has on a confirmed racist, and vice-versa—a nuance not in the original movie. This is about the time I cite Flannery O'Connor's *Wise Blood* as a kind of intellectual precursor for my idea, if you don't look too closely. Although how Enoch Emory following the instructions given by his learned plasma compares to my sewn-together blood brothers is a little hard to explain.

Magda seems fairly dazzled. Her kohl-ringed eyes gleam

and the buttery curls of her perm glow in the subdued light as she sets down her tea. "Will you promise to honor Uncle Lee's intentions?"

Uncle Lee, a double-dealing liar, crook, con man, scheming two-bit hustler who would do anything to get a movie made? Which is to say, a fellow screenwriter.

"Magda," I say, "I'm a screenwriter. I can only honor Uncle Lee's intentions."

The deal is $1,000, which I do not have. For a six-month option, which I do not have. What I have is a great idea for a script and some hope and a couple names.

. . . .

M Y OLD AGENT, MY LAST AGENT, BEN STURGIS, one of the first casualties of the showrunner's revenge, was famous for hiring bright assistants. They came and went like Spinal Tap drummers because they kept getting plucked away by management companies and talent agencies. While I was still represented, I paid attention to them, possible future studio heads. My favorite was Candy Kwang. Her given name was Teresa, but she understood the virtues of alliteration in that world. She was an Immaculate Heart grad and, like most Immaculatas, understood the value of the well-written word, which is to say she'd been a fan of my work. I'd stayed in touch when I could, congratulating her on a steady upward climb. She was now at Paradigm, a mid-level agent, and doing well.

I didn't want to spook her. She needed to know I wasn't looking for representation—that ship had sunk—just a referral, a hand up if a hand was there. I took a chance. In a business that is conducted 98 percent by phone, I wrote a letter and laid it out. I included the DVD of *The Thing with Two Heads*, my treatment, and an explanation of *why* it would work now.

Candy, bless her heart, remembered me fondly. I had been kind to her, she said in her email, and then she said this: "You can really write, and that still matters. I love your stuff. My boss wouldn't let me sign you, but let me help if I can." And she asked me to lunch. I really must have been kind once. No agent wastes lunch on a writer. This was clearly a handout, but I wasn't going to turn it down.

. . . .

MUSSO-FRANK'S HAS ONE ROW OF BOOTHS IN the old room where you can hear yourself think, the inner row. The best of these is closest to the grill. Candy had snared one of these two-toppers and was waiting, well into a dirty martini. She'd always been pretty in that Catholic school girl way. Now, even dressed down, she was gorgeous. One side of me wished we were on the outer showcase row of booths. I sighed and sat. My luck was holding. Pedro, our waiter, remembered me from long ago. I ordered what I always order when someone else is paying—a martini, shrimp cocktail (only suckers order the crab, which is canned), asparagus with hollandaise as an appetizer, filet mignón rare with béarnaise, Lyonnaise potatoes, and a good glass of Bordeaux to go with that. Candy ordered the Caesar and sweetbreads with a choice pinot noir. We had our toast, and she got right into it.

"Who is your ideal pitch?"

"An actor who wants to direct."

"Why?"

"Because this project is bulletproof."

"How?"

"Because it doesn't matter who you cast."

"Explain."

"The dream version would be Kevin Hart and put Mel Brooks on his shoulders. That one would write itself and open at fifty million. But it doesn't *have* to. It doesn't need stars. The first time around it was about the white guy. Not this time. This time it's about the white guy learning something from a Black guy who has been on death row.

"Make it Cedric the Entertainer. Whoever is on his shoulder, first time that white guy tells him where he wants to go, Cedric the Entertainer looks down his nose and says, 'Back off. You best remember who's running this ship. I'm not just the Mayflower, Pilgrim. I'm the fucking captain of the Mayflower.'

"But the point is, it can work with *any* good Black comedian. It could work with Redd Foxx, any of the Kings of Comedy. It could work with Godfrey Goddamned Cambridge. It doesn't matter.

"And the white guy, same thing. It could work with Carroll O'Connor, Archie Bunker to the American public. For God's sake, it could work with Pat Boone. You could even *do* the sex scene. Picture Pam Grier yanking off the pillowcase, Pat Boone's eyes rolling back in his head. Pam says, 'that boy is having too much fun.' Maybe Pat starts singing like James Brown—please, pleease, pleease, please—or at least a little more like Elvis."

Candy was laughing now. "I think I may have the guy for you."

We order more martinis.

• •

IT TOOK A LITTLE LONGER FOR CANDY TO ORGANIZE the meeting than we figured it would. The comedian slash actor was definitely interested in the project, but he was also interested in Candy, which complicated things. Every time Candy tried to schedule a meeting, it seemed to be contingent on a date.

Since I signed the non-disclosure agreement, I can't say exactly who he was. I'll just narrow it down by saying he was one of the young, short, tubby, white comics, but not the nebbishy one, more the aggressive one. His production company had scored a studio deal, and they were throwing money, so far with nothing to show for it.

The comedian/actor definitely wanted to add that second slash to his résumé and become a C/A/Director, and the bonus in my project was the possibility of working with Black comedians/actors, apparently a glaring omission from his résumé.

None of this meant that we—the C/A and I—would actually meet, but after three readings, two by interns and one by staff, we had reached Marshall, the C/A's head guy. If Marshall said yes, we were in. Or, as the C/A put it, with one of his signature lines, "I'm partial to Marshall." Marshall was a busy boy. He set up and canceled two meetings in February, but before he went on vacation set a definite and what he called a "pro forma" meeting for March 15. "I like what I've read," he told Candy. I needed to hear that. I wasn't selling blood yet, but I had to rewrite two student scripts and picked up an intro class at LACC to make my March rent.

. . . .

ON THE DAY OF THE MEETING, I WAS UN-FASHIONABLY early. It was a nice building on Beverly, not too far from *Jar*; you could lunch at the Farmers Market with a little effort.

I tried to figure out why I felt so much older than everyone else in the room, and I counted the differences.

1. I was the only one with a satchel or anything to carry

paperwork.

2. The only one not wearing tinted lenses indoors.
3. The only one not working on a phone or a tablet.
4. The only one without a cap.

And of course, there was the big one, number 5: The only one actually old. Everyone else was under thirty. The lone exception to this was the kind secretary/ad assist, Julie, who may be closer to my age and is the house mother common to young male production offices. Julie had just brought me my second Smart Water with such solicitude that I was made to feel even older.

I couldn't quite figure out the workspace. No one seemed to be assigned a specific desk, and there were boxes stacked in the hall. I asked the guy on the sofa nearest me, "So, are you guys still moving in?"

He looked up briefly. "Uhh. No." He went back to his text.

I had a surprise for Marshall. It was jumping the gun, but in the last month I'd worked out the first act—actually, almost the first fifty pages of the script, in hand, and it was brilliant. I had the pitch, and he could hear it if he wanted, but if he read the first ten pages and didn't buy it on the spot, he was nuts.

I hadn't shown these pages to Oscar or anyone, but when you know, you know. At my feet, a uniform guy was working his way across the floor, lifting the carpet and gathering taped-down extension cord until he reached the copy machine in the corner. He coiled the cord atop the machine, handed a clipboard for Julie to sign, and then wheeled the machine down the hallway.

Across from me, another bright young intern had turned his cap backward to do FaceTime with an older man who seemed to be snowbound. "Hey, Uncle Jim, thanks for the check. I'm moving back to Pittsburgh for the summer. Yeah. We lost our deal."

Why am I here? That cosmic question had just gotten real specific.

It was about then that Marshall breezed in, and poor dear Julie, who'd been midway between crying and offering me another Smart Water, had to tell him, "Dale Davis is here to see you."

The range of emotions that crosses Marshall's face goes from: *Didn't I cancel?* to *Why didn't I cancel?* to *Where is my gun?* But he recovered, shook my hand, and said, "Give me just a minute to settle in and we'll get started."

Marshall whirled away. I looked around at all the bright young faces staring at their phones and tablets, completely unfazed. They'd all land on their feet, except maybe Julie, who *was* bringing me another Smart Water and tearing up.

"Thanks," I demurred, holding up my still-full bottle. She put it on the table in front of me. "For later."

Marshall bustled out and guided me to his office, which had an impressive view of the parking lot and many blown-up stills of the gummy-faced C/A in action. I understood that Marshall is willing to let the geezer do his full dog-and-pony show, the complete pitch. I didn't need it. I really didn't need it. My hour with Candy let me know I still had entertainment value.

"Can I get you a water?" Marshall said as he pulled out my chair.

I was still standing. "Let's save some time. You're about to close up shop, right?"

Marshall collapsed into his ergonomic device and curled his feet around the pedestal. "Shit, who told you?"

I sat down. "The Xerox guy."

"Damn it." Marshall scrubbed his eye sockets with the heels of his hands and banged his temples. I could see why the C/A liked him; it was one of the more convincing imitations of sincerity that I'd seen lately. "The thing is, I really like your treatment. I think you're on to something. Wherever we land, or, wherever I land, if that's the case, I want to bring you in."

I know my moment. I stood, reached across, and shook

hands. "That would be great." I showed him my water.

I was halfway to the door when Marshall cried, "Wait, wait... You gotta get a shirt. Everybody gets a shirt. I'm very proud of these."

He was back a minute later, holding up a T-shirt. It was a replica of the posters adorning the office. The image was Magritte's non-pipe and below in curled script:

Marshall handed it to me. "All we had left is a small. But it doesn't matter, man. They're collectible. Frame it. They're already up on eBay."

Julie was gone from the desk, and the boys didn't look up as I left. I tossed the shirt into the back seat of the Saturn and tried to decide. Candy wanted me to call, but that was a call I didn't want to make. Not today. I was on Beverly, less than ten minutes from Cedars-Sinai, and I hadn't seen Gus this week. It was on the way home. If I could score street parking, I'd stop.

My first bit of luck for the day: free parking on a side street, so I wasn't out ten bucks for Cedars parking. When I got to the South Tower though, I couldn't find Gus. He wasn't in his room, and nobody would tell me if they'd moved him or if he'd gone to hospice care. I'm not family so they couldn't give me any information.

. . . .

BACK AT HOME, ESMERELDA IS SITTING ON MY steps, and one look told me everything Cedars wouldn't. She's been crying.

She gets up. "Hi, Dale. My dad died this morning." She starts to cry and pretty much collapses in my arms. I get her inside and make some yerba buena tea. She's been here most of the day, handing out envelopes to the tenants, explaining about the rent increases and her father's last wishes. I was the only one left.

The tea revives her a little. "You know what's weird?" Esmerelda says. "I knew my dad was dying. My mom died seven years ago. This morning when they told me, the first thing I thought—I'm an orphan. I'm thirty-three, but I'm an orphan. What's that about? Anyway. I just want to warn you. I don't know what's going to happen. My dad wrote it all out on the rents, but now we don't know what happens on his pension—and my brother and sister are being hard-asses. They want more money. They might even want to sell. I think they got a lawyer. I have to go meet with them, but I wanted to tell you. My dad loved you." She gets up to go.

"Thanks for the warning. Hard times ahead. Maybe I'll utilize Gus's dicho."

"What's that?"

"A folk saying. Down in Nicaragua, whenever Gus got stuck,

when he was really up against it, he'd tell the Nica crew, 'Al Dios rogando y con el mazo dando!' 'Pray to God, then hit it with a hammer.' Always made them laugh."

"I'll get you one of his hammers," she says.

After Esmerelda leaves, I sit down at the computer and do what I need to do—one email to Candy, no details, just letting her know Dadaist Productions lost their studio deal, which might have some effect on whatever charm stubble-boy possessed. If she has anyone else in mind, she knows where to find me.

The second email is to Oscar Grunfeld, and in this one I wave the white flag. "Breakfast at Du-pars?" is the heading. "I'm in trouble" is the message. Du-pars meant I didn't want Jaime Rubin to know, since he's been 86'ed from the joint.

Oscar replied within a minute. "I know. Sol's been bragging. I always enjoy Du-pars. I always enjoy your company. See you at ten tomorrow."

Beware the Ides of March. There was now only the evening and a long night to fill. I knew how to do that. My credit cards can't afford the recompense that this day and Gus deserve, but there's a way around. I have a deal with Roger over at the Tattle Tale Inn on Sepulveda, reserved for the worst nights. I help Roger with his scripts, and in exchange he lets me tend bar. He'd let me sit and drink, but I've told him, I'd rather tend bar. "The deepest human need," I'd explained, "is to feel useful, a requirement not met by my present occupation." Tonight in particular I need the company, and since I pour with a heavy hand, I'll make friends—friends and tips—and all my jokes will be funny. The Dylan Thomas line always gets them: "I'm a drinker with a writing problem." Roger always likes to talk movies after closing. Movies and ex-wives. He has three. We'll get through it.

. . . .

DU-PARS, SERVING REALLY GOOD BREAKFASTS since 1938 at the Farmers Market, Third and Fairfax. Oscar had his first meeting with his agent here in the early '50s. It's dim inside, and the effect is soothing, what I need on three hours of sleep.

Oscar, hyper-punctual as always for these occasions, is in place, ensconced in his favorite red leather booth, attended by our favorite waitress, Sandy G. My coffee is waiting.

As I slide into the booth, she takes away my menu. "Let me guess," she intones, pointing to Oscar, "the legendary buttermilk pancakes, extra syrup for Oski," and nodding to me, "and the eggs Benedict, both traditional and Florentine for Davis."

Eggs Benedict both traditional and Florentine means I get both Canadian bacon and spinach under my poached egg with hollandaise. It is nice to be remembered.

Time to sigh. I've been dreading this moment.

Oscar produces an envelope and hands it to me. "A temporary solution."

Inside is a check for ten thousand dollars. "That is a gift," Oscar says, "not a loan." Not a solution either, but a stopgap and a very Oscar thing to do. "It gives me pleasure," Oscar says, "and you may not remember, but there was a time you helped greatly on a couple of scripts I was stuck on. I think of this as seed money."

"Actually," I tell him, "it's bearing fruit. I'm a third of the way through a full script for *The Thing*... My working title is *Youngblood*."

"That's a shift," Oscar says.

"I'm excited," I say, and I am. "I'm writing four, five pages a day, and it feels really good. I'm a third of the way through."

"Then this is money well spent," Oscar says. "You're in love again."

Dear Oscar. He has a way.

"I had a thought," Oscar says. "Bring me those Bukowski books. I think I have a buyer."

"What?"

"Sol Haverstein is a member of my synagogue. What he did was not just. Not Solomon-like. I'm going to talk to him about that."

This is not the first time that Oscar has summoned F. Scott Fitzgerald's famous line, "The test of a first-rate intelligence is the ability to hold two opposed ideas in mind at the same time and still retain the ability to function." But with Oscar, it's more like four—a confirmed theoretical Socialist in the body of practical functioning Capitalist who is also, as far as I can tell, the leading Macher of his synagogue and the least religious man I know. Which is to say, Reb may be doing a lot of scrubbing on those books.

Sandy G. approaches, orange juices in hands, plates arrayed on each arm, toasts on wrists, entrees on elbows, the Durga of Du-pars. Plates magically descend, levitate, and come to rest, perfectly positioned, just as they would if that multi-armed deity were in front of us.

"Buen provecho," Sandy G. says, "Saha wa hana" and ankles away. The second one, if I remember right, is Jordanian. It's a moment here regulars wait for. She has a rotating stock of gustatory phrases, Armenian and Arabic, Yiddish to Zulu, all essentially saying, enjoy your food. We fade to breakfast.

– "PERSECUTION STREET & HAZARD AVENUE, THE CORNER OF..." –

A STORY BY PHILIP K. DICK
AS TOLD TO D. DALE DAVIS

(2011)

"PERSECUTION STREET & HAZARD AVENUE, THE CORNER OF..."

A STORY BY PHILIP K. DICK
AS TOLD TO D. DALE DAVIS

(2011)

L ETTER FROM THE *ASIMOV FOUNDATION* GLOWING IN the mailbox this afternoon. Mailbox, what a bad description that is >* it is an Apartment Building *Mail Slot*, one of twen-ty-four in my building, hinged door 16-by-6 inches. Mustard is the color. In the 1960s, when all of the apartment buildings in the County of Orange were built, there were only two color options, mustard and avocado. Later came rust. Hinged door,

---

* Regarding > Philip K. Dick's hatred of the semi-colon was well known among his editors and fellow writers. He argued for the cognitive arrow >, which indicated both the closeness and continuation of subject matter, unlike the interruptive ; which is neither fish nor fowl, neither pause nor stop.

vertical oval slots, louvers really, through which I can see the envelope. Crisp, textured, 120# parchment paper, letter-press imprinted return address, my name and address in calligraphic India ink. French slash through the 7 in the zip. Dumped on top, but at the wrong angle, are the usual circulars and bills.

I turn the key and let the door drop down. I pick up the "usual" mail with my left hand and apply tongs to the envelope. Side by side, nose-high, they definitely smell different. The "usual" smells usual, that particular dioxide odor, the must of landfills, of paper confined in plastic bins. The Asimov letter smells different, a light odor of lilacs and Egyptian cotton blown on a clothesline. No postal worker has touched this envelope. I do not trust the Post Office, but I trust their habits and their odors. Also, the Asimov letter does not pass the eye-test > it is too crisp and composed. Until today, I have not had a letter in sixteen years that did not bear the signature crinkles and crenellations of governmental inspection, steamed opening, and resealment.

I drop the "usual" mail into the receptacle of the landlords and carry the envelope, via the tongs, to my darkened apartment, and there, behind the tinfoil-shrouded windows, set the Revere Ware tea kettle on the largest stove coil, and turn the burner to ten. In three minutes, I have steam, which I apply to the flap of the envelope. Tongs again, and I withdraw the letter and flatten it on the kitchen counter to peruse.

Salutation is the usual, *Dear Mr. Dick*, and the opening paragraphs are also the usual blather, *Yr long distinguished career, yr cntributns to the wndrful wrld of sci fi anonanon.* I scan down to the bottom lines. Yessums indeed! They want to give me money!

Scan, scan down to the contact. There is a number there, 555-666-1977, and a name, Mr. Richard Phillipps. Got to be kidding. Beast of the Year. Current year of the Beast, my name reversed.

Wrong as rain!

I lift the letter with the tongs and hold it over the desk lamp. The periods at the ends of two crucial sentences in the text:

We would like to relieve you of all financial anxieties. And *You deserve this.*

seem overlarge and slightly bulbous. I suspect micro-dots.

My neighbor, Charles Freck, has the electron microscope I need. Charles Freck works for the school district of the County of Orange when he can. He told me he has the microscope on a loan. What Charles Freck actually said was, "It was *a* loan. It was alone so I grabbed it, so I grabbed it." And then he actually said, "Heh-Heh" and "Heh-Heh," just like in a comic-book, with pauses. He is a horrible human being. Sadly, one of the few I can trust. It doesn't matter. I have the key to his apartment.

You have to kick your way through the McDonald's burger wrappers and Styrofoam clamshells to reach the drafting table, also on loan, on which the microscope sits.

I find two glass slides and mount the letter between them, right on those exaggerated periods. Lights off. Scope light on and focus. The first, larger dot, under 1500x magnification, reveals this: *No Aphids were harmed in the composition of this letter.*

Shift to the second, smaller period: *Just joking, Jerry.*

So. A fan, somewhere in the works. Bodes well. I leave Charles Freck's door completely open so that the rest of the complex can share my disgust and walk to the Union 1776 gas station on Ball Road where resides the only pay phone that I trust. I drop a quarter and dial the given number. The plummy voice answering "Asseemoff Foundayshun" is in that fruity mock-British accent so currently favored in corporate world. I respond in kind, through my surgical mask, with my Soupy-Sales puppetry voice: "Mister Dick's secretary, calling for Mister Richard Phillipps. Is Mister

Phillipps available." It is not a question.

"One moment, one moment," she replies. "Let me see if Mr. Phillipps is available. Can you hold?"

"Of course," I reply in my high, screechy twitter. "I am holding." Bouncy music fills my ear. "Yeah the worst is over now / The morning sun is breaking like a red rubber ball."

A pleasant baritone voice breaks in: "Dick Phillipps here. We've been anticipating your call ... Mr. Dick?"

"Can you hold," I screech.

"Of course," he replies.

Advantage mine. I let the traffic sounds of Ball Road, the distant murmur of Disneyland, and the sharp clang of bells as cars cross the rubber air hoses of the gas station summoning attendants, fill his ears. Then I shut the door of the phone booth, lift my surgical mask, and exhale through cupped hands into the receiver, "Hooooaaaahhhhhhh," then a pause, then, "Philip K. Dick here. How may you help me?"

"Oh, Mister Dick," he says with genuine or excellently feigned warmth. "We are so glad to hear from you. Your time is valuable > I won't waste it. We would like to immediately send you a cashier's check. Twenty-five thousand dollars. No strings attached, as proof of our good intentions, and then we would like to fly you to our offices to discuss how we might help you further."

A good start—I maintain silence. "Mister Dick? Sir?"

"Send the check," I say. "You have the address. If the check is good, then we will talk again." Usually, this is where I would slam down the receiver, but I've learned. I cut the coiled silver-armored cord with my compound bolt cutters and drop the receiver into my pack.

It's a short walk home, but by the time I get there, another Asimov Foundation envelope glows in my empty mail slot.

The check, I learn the next morning at my local Robber Baron bank, is indeed legitimate. By the end of the day, most of the 25K will be siphoned off to back child support, arrears alimony, and back-tax liens, but for the moment I am financially confident. I even treat Charles Freck to lunch at Bob's Big Boy and listen to his complaints of mysterious intruders in his apartment who have further mystified him by stealing nothing > instead, several bags of trash were hurled onto his couch.

As we pass the 1776 gas station, I note that the phone has already been repaired, so I know better than to use it again. Freck returns to what he calls work—a janitor, hoping to work up to A/V specialist. Back home, I utilize Freck's phone. Richard Phillipps is on the line in a nanosecond.

"Mister Dick." The warmth in his voice could sustain a thousand Hallmark specials. "Mister Dick, we are so glad to hear from you. Before you hang up today, I'm going to give you my direct line so that you can avoid the switchboard in the future. But right now, I'd like to see how soon we can fly you to the foundation."

No need to check my calendar > unscheduled days stretch into what we call the future like stairs in an Escher print. But what I say is, "I'm in the middle of numerous edits on many books. How long will this take?"

"What is the most convenient airport for you?" If I could somehow gather up Phillipps's voice, I think I could get a good night's sleep on it. So soft and warm. "We really want to make this comfortable for you. The plane is circling the area right now. You just decide where you want us to land. Which airport would you prefer to fly from: Fullerton, Santa Ana, or Anaheim?"

Worrisome. I have no idea which is best. I never knew there were airports in those cities. Never one to give up any advantage, I make the choice. "Anaheim," I say. "After all, that is where I live, as far as you know."

"There is a car waiting outside your complex, Mister Dick. The driver's name is Ivan. We look forward to finally meeting you." The dial tone seems celebratory.

Outside is one of those Lincoln limousines with darkened windows. When I step out of the entryway, the driver pops out. His arms are up, and he rounds the car, flinging open each door, to let me know it is empty and safe. He is a short man, bald and blinking like he's just been wakened from a nap. I assume he was picked for this assignment for a reason.

"Tell me your name."

He reaches into his coat pocket and brings out a post-card-sized card. "IVAN," it reads, and below in smaller italic print: *I was told not to talk unless you wished me to.* I slide into the leather-scented back seat. "Drive on, Ivan."

It's a short ride to the airport, an airport five minutes from my apartment, which I never knew existed. There is a whole world out there we know nothing about unless we are pilots.

A small, sleek jet is waiting. Ivan guides me to the stairway and hands me off to a lithe young woman wearing a uniform that looks like a copy of the ones the stewardi wore in *2001*. She reaches down—she is much taller than me—takes my hand, and guides me aboard. There is only one seat, and she buckles me in. Liftoff is instantaneous. As I sit, we accelerate. We sweep out over the ocean—glorious view—and then circle around to, I believe, San Bernardino. By now the sun is almost down. I watch the sunset from my chartered jet. Darkness descends. Soft lights come on in the cabin. I am offered champagne, liquors, liqueurs, beer, soft drinks. I believe I am offered drugs. I decline. I maintain. I sip the mineral water I've brought with me and wait for the Darvon I took at home to kick in. We begin to descend. I can feel the shift in the small of my back. We touch down in Burbank. It seems like a long flight for such a short distance, but my sense of time has been fluctuating lately. Waiting behind the plane is another Lincoln limo and a driver flinging open all the doors, as before, who looks surprisingly like Ivan. "I am Ivan's brother, Ivor," he tells me. "Are we now building trust?"

I get in. The slip of paper with my name that I had wedged under the ashtray in the back seat is missing. So, the car has been cleaned, or this is a different car. "Drive more, Ivor," I say. We glide across Burbank, pass Warner Brothers, and shoot up Barham, down Cahuenga, and into the heart of Hollywood. Tourists attempt to peer through the darkened windows.

Ivor turns down a side street, turns twice more, and heads into a cul-de-sac I don't know > at the end is the wide entrance to an underground parking garage. We dip, descending through a narrowing aperture that continues to narrow like a funnel. One hundred feet beyond the entrance, the walls close in and seem only inches from the sides of the car. Through the darkened rear window, I can make out what I think are metal blast doors descending to block the passage behind us. I continue stabbing at the leather seat beside me with the honed needle tip of my retractable ballpoint pen, completing my name in punctures imperceptible to the untrained eye. I finish the second *k* just as we leave what I now know to be a tunnel and enter a vast shadowy vault that feels circular. We ease to a stop in front of an elevator. The doors open. It must be a freight elevator, enormous, and it's packed like a clown car. There must be forty people in there, all wearing what look like lime-colored safari suits, except for a tall man in a double-breasted brown suit who is smiling warmly at me. Richard Phillipps, I presume. I click closed my needle pen and step out of the car. Phillipps's minions, meanwhile, have fanned out in a semicircle on either side of the elevator, and when they see me, they break into what must be practiced applause. Phillipps steps forward, shakes my hand, and guides me to the elevator, and they continue to applaud as the doors close on just the two of us. The elevator buttons have no numbers or letters that I can see, but a quick estimate of the number of buttons would make this the tallest or deepest building in Los Angeles.

Phillipps pushes eight or nine buttons in a sequence too quick for me to master, and the elevator moves, and at first, it seems to move sideways, judging by the way the sound of the applause from the garage shifts. Then we seem to ascend, but after a long while, I can't decide if we are ascending or descending. Then, slowly, the doors open to what is either a stunning view of Los Angeles from an enormous height, or one of the best back-screen projections I've ever seen. I fix my gaze on a couple of key points, traffic lights on Sunset, the neon façade of Grauman's Chinese Theater. If it's a loop, I'll know by the sequential repeat.

"Mister Dick," Richard Phillipps intones. "Mister Dick. What an honor! This will be very brief, just a few documents for you to initial and sign, and we will be giving you the first of what we hope to be many bi-monthly checks, and then send you on your way. We don't want to be held responsible for changing the course of world literature through any bookkeeping delay."

Better and better. Usually, the cocksuckers want to sit about and talk *literachah* before they sprinkle my crumbs. I once had to sit through a three-hour luncheon and listen to some professor geezer refer to me as "the poor man's Pynchon."

I was still concentrating on the light sequence, which meant I hadn't said anything to Phillipps or even looked his way. He came and stood in front of me, blocking my view and ruining my running count on the sequence. "Is everything all right?" The warmth and concern he was able to project was startling. I wondered if it might be chemically induced.

"Oh yeah," I say. "Hunky-dory. Copacetic. So that's it? I don't even have to meet up with Ike?"

"Ike?" He does baffled pretty good too.

"Ike. Isaac. Isn't this his way of apologizing for that stuff he said about me?"

"Oh—oh dear. You've misunderstood. This is the *Roger* Asi-mov Foundation. No relation, as far as I know. Our Mister Asimov is simply a patron of the arts."

He lays out the papers on a long, low table in front of the window or back-screen and hands me a pen.

I look at him. "I prefer to use my own pen." I bring out the Needle-Master, rotate the barrel, and click, bringing down the roller-ball chamber filled with disappearing ink. I've used it for years. Freck's formula, that ink, won't actually disappear for twelve hours—then, untraceable.

I don't bother reading the boilerplate in front of me, since in twelve hours they won't own a valid signature. I just initial and sign where he points. He gathers the documents and shakes my hand again, palpable warmth that almost vibrates, radiates from his hand. Definitely something chemical going on there.

"I'll take these to the vault and then return with your check. Meantime, I'm going to turn you over to one of my colleagues, Mr. Cavitage, who will outline the health insurance and investment programs we're setting up for you."

Elevator doors slide open. Phillipps steps on, and out steps a tiny, rigid figure in a blue terry-cloth leisure suit. The man is about the size of a ten-year-old boy, less than five feet tall > he's braced, leaned forward like he's walking against a hurricane. His face reminds me of a hood ornament, the Pontiac Chieftain, all beaky nose and slanted forehead. He actually looks like a ferret on steroids and speed, and his smile is a fixed rictus.

He circles me, casting for my scent. His head jerks back and nods, nostrils flared. He does not like what he smells. I see rage and loathing in his small red eyes, which are completely round. I turn with him as he circles me and then blinks. "Cavitage?"

"It's Jesper." His voice is a strangled high-pitched keen, like a trampled jockey's. He doesn't blink. That wasn't a blink that I saw. I can't be sure, but he may have a nictitating membrane. There's a flash of something inside the eyes, like a camera shutter. I am extremely grateful that the massive dose of Darvon I ingested before I got on the mini jet has finally kicked in.

"Cut to the chase," he almost sings in his helium-high voice. I haven't heard such clamped violence directed at me since my father died and my daughters stopped talking to me. He pulls out some instrument, like a garage door opener, and presses a button. A blue light flashes and the windows turn a shimmering white. They *are* back-screens. I instantly realize that I have no idea whether I am above or below ground or even what city I am in. They could have used the same technology on the windows of the limo.

Jesper/Cavitage presses another button, and a montage unfolds on the eight screens that surround us.

We watch in silence as sheaves, reams of dated prescriptions, roll down the screens, followed by date-marked videos of me presenting those prescriptions to numerous pharmacies throughout the County of Orange, all the same drug, all the same day. This montage spans months, eventually years. I look the same in every scene, thrusting forward the script, twitching, blinking. The pharmacists' obverted gazes and resigned nods are equally similar. There is no musical soundtrack to this, but it feels like there is.

Then a dissolve and a shift, more videos, but more jarring. All in my bedroom, all on my bed or the tiny trampoline next to it—Kathy in half her Santa Ana High School cheerleading outfit, Linda in her unbuttoned Girl Scout uniform, Susan in the Mouseketeer gear, all statutorily date-marked. And again, like the pharmacies, I look the same in every scene, twitching, blinking. Another dissolve, and the next images are stills, black and whites, heavily flashed like old crime-scene photos—Molly sprawled next to the toilet, where she either OD'd or stroked out. She wasn't found there > she was found blanket-shrouded on a bus bench on Harbor Boulevard, but the photos of me, grasping her ankles, preparing to hoist, as always, blinking, twitching, will make any DA drool.

A final montage now crawls all eight screens. The documents I signed perhaps ten or fifteen minutes ago—perception is always a problem, isn't it—now highlighted with bold-faced type indicate that for the sum of $25,000—flash of canceled check—I seem to have signed away the rights to all my published works and/or future works, in perpetuity.

"One more thing," Jesper pipes triumphantly. "That ink's not going to disappear or even fade. Charles Freck has been co-operating with us for quite a while. Quite a while." One final image assembles on the screens: Charles Freck in slow-motion, turning to face the camera, whipping his hand to his hip like a B-movie gunfighter and raising a fist and then middle finger to me. "Face-Ass," he clearly mouths, his favorite saying. The screens fade back to shimmering white and then dim to gray.

"And to think," I murmur, "people have accused me of being paranoid."

Jesper giggles > it's like listening to a raccoon trill. "Yeah, paranoids have enemies too you know."

"Delmore Schwartz once said that." I seem to still be in murmur mode.

"Yeah," Jesper sniggers, "and he's dead too."

"What do you want?"

"Not my department," Jesper says. "I'm Stick. You need to speak with Mister Carrot."

On these words, the elevator doors slide open. Why do I feel as though it never left? Phillipps steps out, roseate as ever, and Jesper steps on. He looks up at Phillipps. "You got those trainees assembled? I feel like a good game of hide-and-seek. With pistols. Bang! I see you!"

The elevator doors come together, just like the hands that applauded me in the parking garage. "Toodle-oo," Jesper trills. The elevator does seem to descend, trailing the "ooooooh...."

"Well," Richard Phillipps says brightly, "on to happier scenarios!"

"Can I just go home? You can keep the money."

"Oh, Mister Dick, we've moved far beyond those parameters. If I even thought about doing that, I know that Mr. Cavitage would send those videos and receipts to your parole officer. That's just who he is and what he does.

"Let's look on the bright side. Yes, you may be here a while, but is that such a bad thing? All your needs will be attended to. We have a twenty-four-hour pharmacy here > you call, they deliver. Medical care, meals, companionship available from the same phone. All we ask of you is your writing and editing skills. There is an end in sight, and you will be very well paid."

Sunlight isn't that important to me, and the whole deal doesn't sound much different from what I endure with most editors and publishers. He's lying about the money, of course, but if the pharmacist is simpatico, this could all work. "What do I have to do?"

"It's some editing work." Phillipps is beaming now that I'm in his grasp. "Our benefactor, Roger Asimov, had several favorite writers. You were one. There was another, a man who enjoyed commercial success in his lifetime but never achieved the critical acclaim he yearned for."

If I'm reading this right, I get to resuscitate some forgotten Knut Hamsun and go home. Yeah, I can do that. Why am I being so reasonable? Is this the Darvon talking?

"This author," Phillipps intones—*Danger! Danger! Anytime anyone says "Author" there is danger ahead. Same as Physician or Attorney, inflated words for Doctors and Lawyers. Agenda ahead!*—"This author left behind a last, uncompleted work. The large picture is complete, but it needs to be sketched in. Some blanks need to be filled."

Phillipps is striding and gesturing now. His conviction is wonderful. "I think of this project as very much akin to the unfinished manuscripts of the commercially successful but critically savaged fantasist, Robert E. Howard, whose life and work was restored, validated, and finally appreciated by critics because of the posthumous efforts of L. Sprague De Camp and P. Schuyler Miller—*I am still listening here but going a little walkabout. What is it about science fiction writers that compels us to use ornately formal and initialed names? No Bob Howard, no Bob Heinlein. It's Robert E. Howard, Robert A. Heinlein, H. P. Lovecraft, A. E. Van Vogt, Arthur C. Clarke, Ursula K. Le Guin. Do we so seek dignity and cultural approval? If I survive this, I will henceforth publish as Phil Dick!*—Conan the Barbarian lives on because of their efforts, and we believe you can do the same and bring the deserved critical acclaim that was withheld in this author's lifetime."

Darvon is, or I am, agreeable. "Point me the way."

Phillipps beams. "Let me show you to the library." Screen seven pops toward us, and a door and corridor are revealed. The corridor is narrow, brushed aluminum. I feel as though I'm walking through a passageway on a ship. At the end is a red leather door, which pops open with a hiss. The door has rubber seals, like those on watertight compartments, but beyond is a cozy room, with armchairs, where a glowing fake fireplace awaits. There is a mantelpiece with a frozen clock. There is an actual roll-top desk, with a green felt-topped platen. A long table to the side holds what look like manuscript cases. On the platen is an open manuscript. Olivetti typed, if I am any judge, on onion-skin paper.

Phillipps scrubs his hands uncontrollably. "I'm so excited. I feel like William Mulholland when they opened the floodgates from the Owens Valley. Like him, I can only say, Mister Dick, there it is. Take it! Drink from it! The phone inside the clock will bring you anything you need. I leave you to your joyous task."

The door hisses closed behind him. I test it. There is a definite air-lock seal. No time like the present. I sit down at the desk and flip back to the first pages of the open manuscript.

They say that Judas, at the end, realizing what he'd bought into, tried to give the money back. Well so did I. Judas, unlike me, was brave and could do the right thing. The result will be the same, but I will go out with a whimper, not a bang like Judas. It will take a long, long time for me to braid my noose.

I stare down again at the first page:

-- 1 --

RESCUE EARTH

(WORKING TITLE):

A NOVEL IN 10 VOLUMES

BY

L. RON...

– PAYDAY –

(2012)

PAYDAY

(2012)

THESE ARE THE SEVEN T-SHIRTS THAT JAIME RUBIN
has modeled for us in the last week.

On Sunday, he flaunted a Ferrari red job with a clunky,
iron-on Jack Daniel's bottle. The script: *No Pain? No Pain!*

Monday's child was a French's mustard yellow flamer with
crimson lettering: *A Self-Made Man is about as Possible as a Self-
Made Bed!*

Tuesday: Teal blue and Buccaneer orange: *Street Dumb!*

Wednesday: A shiny, black plasticized shirt with iron-on
white lettering. Looks like a trash bag sprayed with Silly String:
*How do you know when a Teamster has died on the set? Usually,
the donut drops out of his mouth!*

Thursday, Jaime's favorite: *I hit the Glass Yarmulke!*

Friday was silver and black: *Just Whine, Baby!*

And Saturday, a light, self-indulgent puce with chrome lettering: *Blogs Are for Blurning!* Jaime doesn't usually display such
an orderly sequence. Usually, he will wear the same T-shirt three
or four days in a row.

What happened was this: Jaime picked up a *New Yorker* at
the library and found a cartoon that should have been his. One
of those anonymous cartoonists, probably Ziegler, who always
remind you of someone better. The cartoon shows a drunk

sprawled on a bus bench, beer bottle in his slack fingers, and his T-shirt says *No Pain? No Pain!* Jaime was furious. It was one of his signature lines; he'd invented the phrase more than a decade ago but had nothing but anecdotal proof.

Jaime's first thought was that he should establish copyright, but that turned out to be expensive, or more than Jaime wanted to pay, so he invented the new and revised poor man's copyright.

Every morning this week, Jaime has put on a different T-shirt of his own manufacture and then had me photograph him holding up a copy of that day's *Los Angeles Times*. It's the kind of thing that blackmailers do. I suggested a one-day shoot, after the first two days. I didn't see why I should have to get up every morning like I was going to work when I was only helping Jaime. The important thing, I argued, was the date displayed in the newspaper. Jaime said the daily ritual appealed to his sense of order. "Art," Jaime told me, "is making order out of chaos. I provide the chaos."

Each of those shirts has a history and is designed to provoke a target group. *No Pain? No Pain!* Jaime tried to flog that shirt at Al-Anon, Narc-Anon, and every other twelve-step meeting he could find. He never got beat up, but he did get doused with a lot of over-boiled coffee. He tried to sell the *Self-Made Man* shirt at Libertarian Conventions and Ayn Rand Worship Gatherings. Not a lot of humor among those crowds. There he did get beat up.

Street Dumb! was the result of a furious series of unpublished letters to the editor at the *LA Times*. Jaime took exception to articles that confidently used a current catchphrase. Donald Trump, Al Gore, Samuel L. Jackson, and politician Gloria Molina were all described as "street smart" by the *Times*. Jaime argued that it was a bad use of language, a loose and inaccurate description, and he insisted that if it was a genuine term then the *Times* would also use the concomitant term: *street dumb*.

He provided an example, describing the director of the *Times*'s editorial pages, Andrés Martinez, as street dumb. Perhaps even freeway dumb. None of these letters were published, even under appeal, and the paper's ombudsman eventually banned Jaime from the paper's email system. All further communications from Jaime were designated spam.

Life sometimes imitates art. The Teamster's joke always provoked hidden laughter and threats on any set, but a few Teamsters actually bought the shirts—the only sales Jaime ever made as far as I know—and wore them proudly. *Just Whine, Baby* offended notoriously sensitive LA and Oakland Raiders' fans, and *Blogs Are for Blurning!* pretty much pissed off anyone under thirty. Jaime's hit single, the one T-shirt that guaranteed that he would be screamed at, was the ever-effective: *I Hit the Glass Yarmulke!*

I actually saw him being screamed at on the occasion of the shirt's debut. He had persuaded me to join him with his breakfast circle at the Farmers' Market on Fairfax and Third, where Jaime broke wind and fast with another group of elderly and faded TV and screenwriters.

Jaime was just raising a bagel with a smear to his lips when he was confronted by an Israeli tourist, a gorgeous Sabra who looked like she'd just come back from desert combat. She was tanned, freckled, with coils of reddish hair, and she skidded to a stop in front of Jaime to reread his shirt, then she plucked the bagel from his lips and held him by the ear. "Are you an anti-Semite?" she asked. Her voice had a sexy rasp. Jaime, retelling the story always interjects here, "Mein Gott, the arms on that woman. She had raised veins bigger than any of my muscles."

Jaime, still in her grasp, said, "No. I am not an anti-Semite. I am a screenwriter, and if you are a screenwriter in this town, to reach the highest levels, you must be MOT." Jaime was on his toes by now, as she lifted him to eye level.

"MOT," she said. "What's MOT?"

"A Member of the Tribe," Jaime said. "And I am not MOT. I am ROT, Rest of the Tribe. I am Sephardic. Sephardim."

She dropped him like an insect, staring, hands curled like she should swat him. Jaime scuttled. As she flexed a bicep, Jaime was already under the table and churning away on all fours, hidden by the enormous white legs of Midwestern tourists slimming down with platters of fish and chips at Tusquellas.

The only other time I ever saw Jaime that nonplussed was also at the Farmers' Market, when he was confronted by a woman wearing a superior T-shirt. Jaime was wearing "Just Whine, Baby!" when a nice but rugged-looking woman wearing Raider gear, mid-thirties, dirty blonde, stopped at his table. "That's lame," she said. "That's not even a real T-shirt." She slowly unzipped her Raider jacket and flashed Jaime with her shirt, also silver with black lettering. *Beat Me, Fuck Me, Make Me Write Bad Checks!* Jaime came close to groveling. He acknowledged her win. "That T-shirt," Jaime said, "could eat my T-shirt."

The thing about Jaime is that he seems to like abuse, or at least attention. He's not delusional. This is not Melrose Larry Green or Angelyne; Jaime is not going to peddle the *Socialist Worker* or sell autographed breastprints, but he does like attention or abuse.

Jaime assumes punishment is a given, a tradeoff, relishes the abuse, and leaves his mark. He entertains and stays in your memory. Jaime's other quality, the main reason we put up with him, is that he is fiercely, stupidly loyal to his friends. He once tried to fistfight a producer who referred to Oscar as a washed-up old Commie. Oscar was touched when he heard about it, but he told Jaime that he didn't understand the business he had chosen, and he was a fool on three accounts. He was a fool because, Oscar said, "I am washed up." He was also a fool because, "I am an old Commie. Not a Stalinist, mind you, but definitely a Premature Anti-Fascist."

"But the main reason," Oscar said, "that you are a fool is that Mednick"—the trust-fund producer Jaime had grazed on the nose—"is the only fool who will hire you. You should be nice to Mednick. He has no taste, but he has the cash." Jaime used his newfound unemployed freedom to picket Mednick's office and invent new T-shirts. *Mednick is a Nudnik* and sold one shirt, to Mednick's secretary.

Today, however, Jaime has made the ultimate sacrifice. The T-shirt he wears is not one of his own. We are at Musso-Frank's, the oldest restaurant in Hollywoodski, and Jaime is wearing a white T-shirt that features the silk-screened cover of my only novel, *Treading Water*. But Jaime, bless him, wears the cover of the German paperback, my one undeniable success.

Wasser Treten, 350,000 copies sold. The twinned elements of competitive swimming and sexual tension appealed to something deep in the German soul. It didn't hurt that a *Der Stern* columnist interpreted my novel as a parable about steroids, which had never occurred to me, since there was no mention of steroids in my text. At the time, I remembered what one of my teachers, Ray Carver, once said: "Be prepared to take credit for anything that anyone reads into your work." The cover was gorgeous: *Wasser Treten*, above a muscular arm and hand, slapping the wall of a pool, a spray of chrome water, feathering to beautifully detailed rainbow beads and droplets.

Musso-Frank's deserves the respect it gets. Yes, it is overpriced by tourist standards, and yes, the staff tends to slight those transients. But for regulars, which I once was, it is a comfort. It is a time capsule. The menu was frozen in the thirties. When I first started coming here, in the 1970s, there were still waiters who remembered F. Scott Fitzgerald, Nathanael West, and Budd Schulberg. Not always fondly. Ferdinand, a tiny, perfectly pressed rooster of eighty, retired as a waiter, but allowed to come in each day, in uniform, and sit at the grill, was displayed and introduced to us literary wimps in 1974. We intoned the name "William Faulkner." Ferdinand responded with something between a shrug and a sneer. "He eat his lamb chops with his fingers."

Musso-Frank's is the one place in town where Jaime is welcomed and even celebrated. He has over-tipped for thirty years and always behaved on the premises, and that goes a long way with the conservative forces that rule Musso-Frank's. Jaime is the only customer I know who can get flannel cakes day or night. He doesn't abuse this privilege, but he will order them to make a point.

Auguste, the daytime maître d', is significantly awaiting us and leads us to the corner booth in the old room, #1, Charlie Chaplin's, the only booth with a window out onto Hollywood Boulevard where there is nothing you want to see, but that is not the point. Clearly, money has changed hands. Auguste is not a romantic. Auguste slides menus to each place-setting as we slide in, and then he nods formally, almost a bow, and says to me, "Congratulations, Mr. Davis. We are very pleased for you." Money has definitely changed hands. Well spent.

Champagne arrives. *Dom Perignon, 1953.* Oscar's favorite, and since he is paying, we drink from the old-fashioned champagne glasses rather than flutes. Jaime raises his glass for the appropriate toast. "About goddamn time," Jaime says.

"Goddamn time," Oscar intones. I nod and sip. It is fairly amazing champagne.

What has happened is something of a miracle. I have not had a screen credit in more than fifteen years. I have not had a television credit, under my own name, in more than ten. Most of my income the last five years has come from rich film students, mostly AFI and USC after I burned my bridge at that Christian college, who needed scripts "organized." I also ghost-wrote biographies for the delusional and taught screenwriting, at a very low level, at three community colleges.

In 1985, my only novel, *Treading Water*, which had sold 1,257 hardback copies in the United States, an accurate accounting of every friend and relative I had at the time, mysteriously became a paperback bestseller in Germany. *Wasser Treten* was optioned by Aleman Studios and the option renewed yearly, for six years, and then went into Limboland, an imaginary place where the option was renewed for minimal fees by accountants who had no idea what was being renewed but wanted to protect the studio's prior investments. This wasn't much money; the only real money was contingent on production. I got a yearly check, smaller each year. The book, the treatment, the first-draft scripts—including one, my then-agent insisted, by Werner Herzog—were kept on file, then in the library, then in the vaults, and then in the basement of Aleman Studios.

And then, twenty years late, the hottest young German director to come out of music videos, Cristophe Brandauer, decided that it was time to shoot the true story of the East German women's Olympic swim team, the Valkyries with chest hair. My novel was about Olympic swimmers, two American couples in a season of competition, leading to an Olympic year. Brandauer's epic was about lesbian couples, steroids, Stasi, and suicide. But he insisted only one title would do: *Wasser Treten.*

My crafty German agent and lawyer, Ernst Muller, now in his late eighties, waited until they had finished production and the title had been published in *Der Stern* and locked in at Cannes, and then he applied for a screen credit in my name. This was the backway in and the only one that would work. The options had lapsed, but the title and my first-draft script were still in the basement. Cristophe Brandauer, *Auteur*, was not about to share screen or story or even title credit with me. It cost Aleman Studios 984,429 Euros to make me go away. Since I was never there, it was easy to make me go away.

Herr Muller took ten percent, which I gladly doubled, and I still ended up, after taxes, with $839,063. Wells Fargo, my bank for thirty-six years, grew so excited by the transfer of funds that they offered free checking. This wasn't like selling a Batman script, but it was more than I'd made on the one novel and three short stories I'd published, and the two produced and twenty-three unproduced but paid-for scripts.

The story made the trades and I've gotten some calls from producers who can't quite remember why they can't hire me and also from Marshall, who does want to talk about the updated version of *The Thing with Two Heads*. Funny what money will do in this town. Particularly undeserved money.

So here we all are at Musso-Frank's, celebrating my payday. Oscar has insisted on shrimp cocktails for the table. He chimes his spoon on his water glass for our attention. "Attention must be paid to these shrimp." It is one of the best things the place does. Their seafood sources are impeccable and secret. Rumor insists that they have their own boat. Three chilled crystal goblets are placed before us, each containing velvety red cocktail sauce flecked with green parsley chiffonade, yellow lemon garnishes, and six plump, pink crustaceans arrayed on the rim. Mexican white shrimp, wild-caught, the best-tasting shrimp in the world.

Oscar presents a shrimp the way a priest offers a host. "I had my first shrimp cocktail at Musso-Frank's in 1948, a boy from the mail room. My first traife, I've never regretted it. I sat at the counter. My boss once sat in this very booth, drinking with F. Scott Fitzgerald. William Faulkner was asleep in the back corner booth with Stanley Rose, who owned the bookstore next door, what is now the New Room."

"Great days," Jaime said reverently. "Great writers."

Oscar snorted. "Both great writers and both of them were terrible screenwriters. They could do a scene. They couldn't do a script."

"How is that possible?" Jaime says. "Wait for it. Wait for it."

Oscar dispenses his standard. "Never send a man to do a boy's job."

We are comfortable, even happy. Oscar orders the Wednesday Special, sauerbraten and potato pancakes. Jaime orders his favorite, the sweetbreads, but for Jaime, they dispense with the jumble of mixed vegetables they call Jardiniere and provide him with sautéed mushrooms and sauce béarnaise. I select the lamb chops—three, not two—with mint jelly, cooked pink, in honor of William Faulkner.

Oscar has brought along two elderly and distinguished California Cabernet Sauvignons from his cellar—a 1959 Inglenook and a 1971 Ridge *Monte Bello*, the wine that shocked the French wine world twice, first in 1976 and again, more triumphantly, in 2006. Musso-Frank's, champagne aside, has usually had a mediocre to terrible wine list. Oscar uncorked these beauties hours ago, at home, and asked for a decanter. Our maître' d', Auguste, decants the Inglenook reverently, pours, and presents the first sip to Oscar, who defers. Auguste swirls, sniffs, sips, and nods, his eyes closing but filled with gratitude. Jaime sighs with his first sip; my response is closer to a moan. Oscar flushes with pleasure.

"One could learn from that wine," Jaime says. "I feel like I've just attended a really good poetry reading. I feel like I've gotten wisdom I couldn't get any other way." He holds up his glass, sighting on the gorgeous ruby sheen left after a swirl, and then he looks at me. He offers not so much a toast, but a challenge. "I am very glad for you," Jaime says. "Don't get me wrong. But we could have done this years ago, except for that union business."

He sips again and speaks again. "So, Norma-Rae," Jaime says. "It didn't work out the way you thought. But we still get the happy ending. Just like at the massage parlor. Once you've paid and paid and paid."

Our meals arrive. The Ridge is decanted and poured into new and larger glasses. Jaime, as he always does, looks askance at Oscar's sauerbraten. "How can you eat that Nazi traife?" Oscar, who lost cousins in the camps and drives a Mercedes 500, does not worry about contradiction. He says, digging in, "It is my childhood. I love it."

"Another self-loathing Jew," Jaime says.

"No," Oscar says thoughtfully, chewing. "It's more like a light dislike."

Jaime, slicing his sautéed thymus gland—the kitchen and waitstaff make sure he gets the more prized heart sweetbread—coating it with béarnaise sauce, is insistent.

"Go ahead. Enjoy the vinegared pork of your oppressors." Oscar holds up a shredded segment of meat, glistening on the tines of his fork. "You can't help your childhood. My mother cooked sauerbraten. We thought we were German. And besides..."Jaime winces. He knows Oscar is bringing up the big guns.

"And besides, as my Aunt Roshelda always said..." Jaime attempts to cover his ears, but it is too late. Oscar breaks into Hebrew *"AL TAAM VARECACH. EN LEHTVACACH."* (All letters in Hebrew are capitalized, or at least that is the way it sounds; you hear every letter.) Jaime davens. Oscar concludes, "Or, as you Sephardim might learn to say, if you ever developed a culture or language: *On taste and smell, one should not argue.*"

Jaime puts down his fork. "That's wise," Jaime says. "That almost deserves a T-shirt."

Oscar does a wonderful silent actor's take, almost rebounding from ignorance or insult. "That's not wisdom," Oscar says. "That is only what my Aunt Roshelda said. She was not a wise woman. I just repeat what she said."

"Well," Jaime says, "I think you underestimate her. I think that is wisdom. Maybe not completely T-shirt worthy, but wise."

Oscar shrugs. "Even a blind squirrel can find his own nuts."

Jaime nearly stands up in the booth. "What did you say?"

Oscar looks at him, mildly startled. "Even a blind squirrel can find his own nuts?"

"Now that," Jaime says, "deserves a T-shirt."

I have been chewing through this, eating my lamb chops with my fingers, smearing mint jelly on them with my fingers, as an homage to William Faulkner, disapproving waiters be damned. A little later, there is a pause. The plates are taken away, the table is cleaned, and we are presented with fresh napkins and cutlery, but the waiters and busboys then hang back. No dessert orders are requested or taken. Clearly, it is time for the toast. Auguste pours the last of the glorious Ridge from the decanter, like a priest, and vanishes, and with him, all waiters and busboys.

The toast, according to Jaime: "You stayed honorable. I have to say, a fool, but honorable."

And Oscar's version: "You come the closest of us all."

I will live with that.

ABOUT THE AUTHOR

LOU **MATHEWS** LIVES IN LOS ANGELES BELOW THE Hollywood sign and is a fourth-generation Angeleno. Married at nineteen, he worked his way through UC Santa Cruz as a gas station attendant and mechanic and continued to work as a mechanic until he was thirty-nine. Since then, he has worked as a freelance journalist, restaurant reviewer, and contributing editor at *L.A. Style* magazine. His journalism has been published in the *Los Angeles Times Magazine*, *L.A. Style*, *Tin House*, *Mother Jones*, *Lit Hub*, and many other outlets—from underground newspapers and airline magazines to corporate house organs like *Bob's Big Boy Family News*. Mathews has published short stories in more than forty literary quarterlies, including the *New England Review*, *Short Story*, *Witness*, *ZYZZYVA*, *Catamaran*, *Chicago Quarterly Review*, and seven issues of *Black Clock*. The stories have been included in more than ten fiction anthologies and two textbook series. He has received a Pushcart Prize, two Pushcart Special Mentions, a Best American Mystery Stories Special Mention, a Katherine Anne Porter Prize, as well as a California Arts Commission and National Endowment for the Arts Fiction Fellowships. He has taught in the UCLA Extension Writers' Program since 1989 and is a recipient of the UCLA Extension Teacher of the Year and Outstanding Instructor awards.

L.A. Breakdown, Mathews's first novel, was published in 1999, when he was fifty-three, and it was picked as a Best Book of 1999 by the *Los Angeles Times*. His last novel, *Shaky Town*, was longlisted for the 2022 Tournament of Books. Lots more information and some videos can be found at https://www.tigervanbooks.com/.

ACKNOWLEDGMENTS

I HAVE BEEN MISREADING A LINE FROM WILLIAM Wordsworth for thirty years. "Child is father of the Man," Wordsworth wrote. Most scholars agree that Wordsworth was saying that who you were as a child will be who you become as an adult. As a teacher, I've always read this line differently. I think it means that as you age, your students should eclipse you and eventually become your mentors. That has certainly happened to me with this book and one previous book, *Shaky Town*. I am forever indebted to Jim Gavin, who made that possible, by creating Tiger Van Books. Go to the website to learn more.

The second person who made this possible is my wife, Alison Turner, who worked a demanding job to provide me with the time to write and rewrite *L.A. Breakdown*, *Shaky Town*, and five other books.

I also have to thank my then-editor at Turner Publishing, Ryan Smernoff, a young man with old-school tastes, who asked the essential question: "You got anything else?" Since then, thanks to my current editors at Turner, Amanda Chiu Krohn and Ashlyn Inman.

Other editors have sustained me over the years that this book was written. First, Steve Erickson, also a friend going back to the early '80s and our days at the *L.A. Reader*. Steve published the title story, "Hollywoodski," "Not Oliver Stone," and "Persecution Street & Hazard Avenue..." as well as four other stories in his deservedly legendary journal *Black Clock*. I owe similar thanks to Josh Tyree, Emily Mitchell, Marcy Pomerance, and Carolyn Kuebler, the excellent editors at the *New England Review* who improved and published "Some Animals Are More Equal Than Others," "Tutorial," and "Desperate Times, Desperate Crimes." I also owe Oscar Villalon, my homeboy from La Puente, who knows where all my bones are buried. Oscar took a leap of faith and published two together—"Individual Medley" and "Oscar"—in *ZYZZYVA*. Lastly, two more recent editors, Catherine Segurson and Elizabeth McKenzie of *Catamaran* and *Chicago Quarterly Review*, are responsible for "Quality of Life" and "Bat Fat."

There are a lot of people in a lot of categories who also helped along the way: My bosses at the UCLA Writers' Program, Linda Venis and Charlie Jensen, Andy Hunter, for various reasons throughout the years, Rob Pettler for loaning me a couple of great lines, J. Ryan Stradal for citing me every chance he gets, Mia Taylor for always being able to explain, Susan Lindheim for tech support, all the members of the home group from 1992 until now, thirty-seven books and counting, and for Matt Sumell who should have known better; you tried, goddamn, you tried.

CREDITS

TURNER PUBLISHING COMPANY

EDITORIAL

PUBLISHER
Todd Bottorff

MANAGING EDITOR
Amanda Chiu Krohn

PRODUCTION EDITOR
Claire Ong

FRONTLIST EDITOR
Ashlyn Inman

LINE EDITOR
Ashley Strosnider

COPYEDITOR
Lisa Grimenstein

PROOFREADER
Marilyn Gillen

MARKETING

MARKETING MANAGER
Makala Marsee

MARKETING ASSOCIATE
Kendal Cliburn

ART & DESIGN

DESIGN DIRECTOR & INTERIOR DESIGN
William Ruoto

COVER DESIGN
M. S. Corley

RIGHTS

DIRECTOR OF RIGHTS
Melissa Schneider

RIGHTS ADMINISTRATOR
Olivia Brothers

PRINTED BY

LAKE BOOK MANUFACTURING

SALES
Bill Elmore

CUSTOMER SERVICE
Corina Blanco

WITH SPECIAL THANKS TO

INGRAM PUBLISHER SERVICES

and all of the people behind the scenes who make it possible to get this book into readers' hands.